MISSION: *impossible to* FORGET

THE IMPOSSIBLE MISSION SERIES • Book Four

JACKI DELECKI

MORE BOOKS BY JACKI DELECKI

THE IMPOSSIBLE MISSION SERIES
Contemporary Romantic Suspense
Mission: Impossible to Resist
Mission: Impossible to Surrender
Mission: Impossible to Love
Mission: Impossible to Forget

THE GRAYCE WALTERS SERIES
Contemporary Romantic Suspense
An Inner Fire
Women Under Fire
Men Under Fire
Marriage Under Fire
A Marine's Christmas Wedding
The Grayce Walters Series Set

THE CODE BREAKERS SERIES
Regency Period Romantic Suspense
A Code of Love
A Christmas Code
A Code of the Heart
A Cantata of Love
A Wedding Code
A Code of Honor
A Holiday Code for Love
The Code Breakers Set

Find all of Jacki's books on her website.
https://jackidelecki.com/books/

ACKNOWLEDGMENTS

Thank you to my "team" who offer their incredible skills and support: Mary-Theresa Hussey, editor extraordinaire; Karuna, my brilliant plot partner; Amy Atwell, who keeps me organized—not an easy task. Thank you.

And to my "home team" who never stop believing in me or my writing: my husband, and my children. Thank you for your continual love and support.

To all Health Care Professionals and First Responders
who are the real life heroes/heroines.
Thank you for your service. Our world is a better place
because of your caring and sacrifice.

CHAPTER ONE

Emily Hewitt swallowed her sobs and fished through her purse for a Kleenex, overwhelmed by the sight of Yuen's casket and the cloying scent of lilies from the massive flower arrangements in the poorly ventilated room. How could Yuen Li be dead?

If she had asked him what was wrong... She might have prevented... If only... Emily couldn't draw air into her lungs. She fixated on a distant spot, one of the flower arrangements with white chrysanthemums, lilies, and red roses. Then she focused on breathing deeply and slowly to distract herself from the raw grief of Yuen Li's parents and his recent bride huddled over the casket.

She and Yuen had just returned to San Francisco three days ago from her Asian concert tour—and that night he had been murdered. She was the last person to speak to Yuen before his body was found at Golden Gate Park. Chills jolted straight up her spine at the imagined vision of the once vibrant man, alone and cold on the damp earth.

Until the police interviewed her, Emily hadn't recognized that Yuen had sounded nervous and how out of character it was for him to ask to come to her apartment. How she wished she had paid more attention to her tour manager's final words, but she had been exhausted from the long flight and excited for her upcoming trip to Seattle.

She had replayed their conversation over and over, puzzled that Yuen had called her so soon after they had said their goodbyes hours earlier at the airport. He asked her if he could swing by her apartment. He joked about wanting to check on Stella, Emily's French bulldog, since the sweet, silly dog might be experiencing jet lag after the thirteen-hour flight from Hong Kong.

Emily continued the breathing practice until she made the mistake of looking again at Yuen Li's casket. She squeezed her eyes shut and focused again on her breathing. She took one breath and then another, falling into the relaxation techniques she used to control her anxiety before a performance.

Her overworked brain couldn't grasp the shock that Yuen was dead. She'd spent four months—stressful, triumphant, and ultimately successful months—performing in China, Singapore, and ending in Hong Kong.

Yuen had been there for her and Stella through the demanding schedule, making her laugh, translating, bridging the cultural differences. He was always excited by her performances, even taking Stella when Emily needed to crash. Without any warning, tears ran down her face when she remembered how Yuen Li had arranged for her to be presented with a cello by the famous violin manufacture, Taixing Fengling Musical Company.

"He was a good man. The random shooting was such a tragedy." Ben leaned closer, his thigh pressing against hers, and squeezed her hand. "Yuen traveled all over the world and was killed for his watch and his new iPhone."

Ben Bellisiano, a successful and charismatic tenor with a voice that had the world at his feet, sat next to her. Yuen Li had also arranged Ben's tours to Asia.

Emily's gaze darted to Ben's. The compassion in his dark eyes and expressive voice might be her undoing. She nodded since words remained blocked between her chest and her throat.

"Let me take you out for a drink after this. We both need it."

Emily pulled her hand into her lap, now unsure if Ben was making his usual moves or was as upset as she was. Knowing how women chased him—and how willingly he let himself be caught— Emily didn't trust Ben's motives in comforting her.

He could have any woman. He *did* have any woman, or so

People magazine claimed. His Mediterranean roots showed in his olive skin, black hair, and Grecian profile, and they made him irresistible. It wasn't his dramatic looks and powerful presence that made Emily susceptible, unlike his hordes of fans. It was the bright, warm timbre of his voice, his soulful passion for the music, his ability to transcend the notes. A gifted artist, Ben should be the perfect match for her.

But the heart was a contrary organ that didn't listen to reason. It was time to wipe the memory of another dark-haired, overloaded, testosterone-filled male from her mind. One who didn't have a voice like a choir of angels but did have a rough bass of a fusillade like the hardened military man he was.

She should accept Ben's offer. After four months, she shouldn't still be thinking of the crazy seventy-two hours she spent with Nick Jenkins and their last night spent in bed. Three days in Sausalito, that's all it was. The only reason the memories flared was because there was a good chance she would run into the drool-worthy man in Seattle. Her older brother worked with Nick, and coincidently, her best friend's boyfriend was Nick's younger brother.

But she refused to cancel her long-planned trip to spend time with Izzy despite the possible awkwardness resulting from that one night of incredible sex—twelve perfect hours of passion she spent with her bodyguard that she couldn't forget. The perfect man, if you were attracted to alpha, domineering men with incomparable bedroom skills…and exceptional ghosting skills.

"A drink is exactly what I need right now."

Surprise flashed across Ben's face before he smiled at her. "I know a bar off Grant Street. We can walk from here."

CHAPTER TWO

Nick Jenkins tilted the wooden chair on its back two legs and observed his marine buddies. The five men displayed the same intense focus on their weathered faces as when they prepped for a mission in the Korangal Valley, though their attention was now directed toward their fellow card players and not their cards. Play the players. Basic Intelligence Training 101.

None of them did anything without laser focus and complete commitment, including a supposedly friendly game of poker between fellow leathernecks. It was this ingrained attitude that made them all hard-ass warriors and the men he trusted to have his six.

The other men took up their positions, fanned out around the makeshift poker table in Logan's condo. Unlike his dumbass brothers, these guys would never betray him.

Treating him like he was a drug addict or an alcoholic, his younger brothers had staged an intervention. The dumb shits tried to tell him, their older brother who'd stepped into the role of patriarch after their father had been killed in action, how to run his life. My God, he used to help his mom change the twins' frickin' diapers. It'd be a cold day in hell when he needed his brothers' advice.

They were lucky that he had jumped on a flight to San Francisco instead of demonstrating that he was still the dominant force in the Jenkins family. He had been training men for over a decade and knew how to use punishing techniques to instill respect.

"When are you going to call the hot cellist? She must have

finished her tour in Asia." Logan threw down his discards, acting as if he hadn't just pulled a firing pin on a grenade.

The shift in the room was subtle, but these men had mastery of all their physical and emotional reactions. Nick had been their team leader and read every tell—the big guy, Tanner, shifting his weight, Logan chewing on his unlit cigar, and the subtle tic above Grayson's right eye. Carter was the easiest to read. When Carter got serious, you knew you were in for some sorry shit. Dylan was the hardest to read, which was why he'd become a spook like Nick's second brother who, fortunately, was always out of the country and not part of the intervention.

"If you're not, I'd be willing to pursue Emily with the big eyes and the big"—Tanner flicked his cards, waiting for Nick to react— "smile."

"I came to hang with my team." Nick smiled at Tanner and ignored the pulse throbbing in his forehead, suppressing the need to grab the asshole by the throat. Emily had fabulous curves, fantastic hills and valleys that he remembered every luscious, mouthwatering inch of. None of the men had forgotten either.

No way he'd give anything to these men. His tell was the tightening in his neck and shoulders and the forward thrust of his jaw. And if he were really pissed off, his forehead vein pulsated.

"And FYI, Emily's not in San Francisco. She's visiting her IT friend, Izzy, in Seattle. You remember, the one who almost got Emily killed."

Nick still wanted to deal some serious damage to Izzy's ex-boyfriend, who had put Emily in North Korean and Russian crosshairs. The fucker would soon be facing trial for treason.

Nick had enlisted these men to help guard Emily four months ago when Emily and her lap dog had been targeted in the event Izzy didn't cooperate by turning over her groundbreaking artificial intelligence work.

Nick had made the major mistake of getting too close to the beautiful and sensitive woman—like in bed too close.

He didn't even try to deny that he couldn't stop thinking of Emily Hewitt, the woman he was supposed to be protecting. The woman who was his close friend's younger sister. The woman he made the big no-no of seducing. The only people who knew how close Nick had gotten to Emily were the men in this room—not his brothers and definitely not Emily's brother. He had promised Emily he wouldn't tell Reeves, but he promptly regretted his promise made under duress—the hot naked kind.

He was an honorable man who followed a code, but not when it came to Emily Hewitt.

"So Emily heads to Seattle and suddenly you appear in San Francisco?" Grayson looked over his cards.

"That's pathetic, man." Logan mashed on his cigar.

"Why would you walk away from a woman like that?"

Dylan discarded two cards.

The list was long. She was young, smart, sensitive, beautiful, with an incredible career. And he was an older, burned-out Spec Forces operative with a hearing loss that would never get better. It wasn't the nine-year difference in their ages. It was that they were worlds apart in life experience. She spent her life creating beauty, and he spent his time bringing death and destruction.

"Who would believe our commander ran from a woman? The man who was respected by the entire battalion is afraid of one tiny woman. Well, she's not tiny. She's a…handful." Logan grinned around the stogie clenched between his teeth.

Nick examined his cards as if they held the NSA's top secrets. He would never show a reaction.

He, like all the men, had total control of his feelings and reactions. It was the only way a soldier survived…until his brothers blindsided him. He was so pissed, he'd told his brothers to fuck off, then flew down to San Francisco to join the men who would never question his ability.

"You know, this is some sorry shit. Look at us. American heroes with nothing to return home to." Grayson was bitter from his contentious divorce. His wife had left him during his last deployment and cashed out his savings.

"Hey, don't look at me. I'm a happily married man." Logan shrugged.

"You're one lucky bastard. I'm not sure what she sees in you." Of all his friends, Logan was the only one married and with kids. Logan seemed to manage the transition from violent deployments to home life with a wife and two great boys. Nick had never kept a personal relationship going for longer than six months. Hell, he'd go that long without seeing his brothers at times.

No, he was doing the right thing avoiding Emily. She was sunshine and light, and he…well, he was darkness and snarls. Avoiding her was the best thing he could do for both of them.

CHAPTER THREE

Nick's phone vibrated in his pocket. He wasn't taking any calls. Nada. Especially from his brothers. But his sense of responsibility meant he had to see who was dialing. Pulling it out of his jeans, he checked the screen. Reeves—Emily's brother, and the company's IT genius. If Reeves was calling to say he had jumped on the "Nick needing a Hawaii vacation" train, Nick was going to dismiss Reeves with the same two words he had used to blast his brothers. No matter who Reeves's sister was.

"What's up, Reeves?" Nick stood and walked to the kitchen, not wanting the men to hear him telling Reeves to fuck off.

"You're in San Francisco, right?"

Nick went from relaxed to roaring pissed. His brothers were now enlisting Reeves to keep track of him. "I'm not working and I'm going to kick Finn's ass for asking you to track me."

"Finn didn't ask me. I tracked you myself."

Nick waited. A highly energetic and verbose guy, Reeves usually jumped right into his concerns. Nick took a slow breath. Had Reeves somehow heard about his marathon with Emily? Had Emily told her best friend Izzy, despite her insistence that he not tell anyone, especially her brother? He understood at the time why she wanted to protect her privacy from her sibling, but now he was uncomfortable around Reeves. Nick felt like he'd betrayed their friendship. There were unspoken rules among men about their sisters.

"You remember how you set up security cameras at Emily's

music studio and her apartment when the North Koreans and the Russians were after her?"

"Yeah. We wanted to see who came knocking after I moved her to the Sausalito safe house."

"Well, both perimeter cameras were disabled sometime in the past twelve hours. And thirty minutes ago, someone tried to break into her studio. They were pros—they disarmed the alarm and unlocked the electronic keypad, but they didn't know who they were dealing with. The sequence set off my backup insurance, triggering the code I had written into the passcode which then—"

Reeves was brilliant, but he could get lost in the details.

"Did they steal anything?" Nick interrupted, not understanding why Reeves had his skivvies in a wad over an attempted break-in of an empty studio. Emily had given up the lease when she'd finished teaching her master classes for the university and left for her Asian tour. And she was supposed to have moved out of her apartment when she returned from her tour. Her agent kept the apartment for clients visiting the West Coast. Emily had planned to go to Seattle, spending the week with Izzy and Reeves, before heading home to New York. Why was Reeves even tracking those former places? Of course, Nick knew Reeves rarely gave up any opportunity to gather information that might protect Emily.

Nick had listened to Reeves and the plans he was making for Emily's visit and knew he had to escape Seattle. Nick heard every detail that Reeves had organized—the tickets to the symphony, the opera, the art museum, the Chihuly garden. And then Nick made his plans—to avoid Emily at all costs.

It was bad enough that he didn't know what he would say or how he would react if he saw her, which, by the way, royally pissed him off. A man known for his mastery of emotions, he refused to apologize for the incredible night they shared. And for a man used to fixing problems, he had no solution for solving his Emily Hewitt obsession.

He calculated that he wouldn't need to see Emily until Izzy and Sten's wedding, which was at least one to two years away. And by that time, she would have a boyfriend or a husband, and his feelings for her would be nothing more than a distant memory. Why did the idea of Emily with another man devastate him more than a bullet wound to the chest?

Reeves's deep voice pitched higher. "And now she isn't answering her phone."

"Take a breath, man. Emily moved out of the studio, right? Did you call the police? They'll report it to the university."

"Are you with her? Is that why she isn't answering her phone?"

The little hairs on Nick's neck stirred. "Emily's with Izzy."

"She's not. She's still in San Francisco. She's flying into Seattle tomorrow."

Nick was trying to keep up with Reeves, but his brain froze. "Emily's in San Francisco?" She was close by. His heart hammered against his chest.

"Her tour manager was murdered three days ago, right after they returned to the States. Emily swore Izzy to secrecy about his death since she didn't want me to 'go all crazy paranoid.' As if I'm paranoid. She is just too innocent to know what shit we deal with. Emily stayed in San Fran for the funeral."

Nick shared a much worse worldview than Reeves, who had never served but confronted evil from behind his computer screen. Another reason why he and Emily were so wrong for each other.

"And the only way I got this information out of Izzy was by telling her about the cameras being disabled and the attempted break-in. You can't think the cameras going down, the break-in, and the murder are a coincidence. Mathematically this is no coincidence. The chances of that occurring are…"

Nick blocked out Reeves's mathematical wanderings. His entire body tightened with the idea of Emily in danger. His experience taught him to be suspicious of any coincidences.

How could Emily be in danger? The only reason she had been threatened before was because of her association with Izzy. Nothing to do with Emily's life as a professional cellist. Nick wanted her to have a safe and wonderful life. It was the reason he walked away from her. To keep her safe from the likes of him. He thought of himself as the biggest risk she faced.

"What do you know of the murder?" Nick lowered his voice, reining in his reactions and Reeves's escalating panic.

"I'm hacking into the police report now. But Emily told her that it was a burglary gone wrong. Emily had to give a police interview since she was the last person to speak with Yuen Li. Why wouldn't she confide in me? Emily should have called me. I could've flown down and helped her."

"Reeves, she's a grown woman who travels all over the world. She is very capable and wouldn't want your help." Nick was having the same thoughts—why hadn't she called him? He had told her he would always be available to help her before he walked away without any further contact.

"But damn it. She's a musician. She doesn't know anything about murder and police interviews. I should've gone with her."

Reeves was right. Emily was a very sensitive woman. She must have been overwhelmed by the loss, and then a police interview? The only interviews Emily gave were for NPR and the *New York Times*.

"Have you tracked her phone?" Nick needed to know where she was.

"It's dead. But I checked in with Charles, her usual driver, and he said he was scheduled to pick her up at a bar on Grant Street. Emily barely drinks. And now Charles isn't answering his phone either."

Used to remaining calm in a crisis, Nick felt panic grow. He called upon his years of experience in leading men into battle. "Emily always forgets to charge her phone. You know that, right? Probably with the stress of the funeral, she forgot to plug it in."

Reeves chuckled. "You're right. I swear my sister would forget to get dressed—"

Nick shut down the vivid flash of a naked Emily laughing as they ate carryout on the bed. "Have you or Izzy hacked into the camera feed of the bar?"

"Already on it. No cameras. It's a dive. Not a place that my sister would willingly go into. And the street cameras aren't focused on the entrance."

"I'm heading to the bar now. Text me the address. And if your sister is having a drink in the bar, I'm going to kick your ass."

"Thanks, Nick. I owe you." Nick hung up. Reeves would never owe him. Not for taking care of Emily.

CHAPTER FOUR

"What time is your flight tomorrow?" Ben took Emily's elbow and steered her toward the exit. The bright lights of the garish Chinatown bar glared off Ben's angular face.

After the excruciating interaction with Yuen's parents and widow after the service as Emily tried to comfort them, she knew she'd made the right decision to have drinks with Ben. He was good company, amusing her with his tour debacles and his groupies' escapades. Neither spoke of Yuen or the funeral.

"Early." She yawned widely. The jet lag had hit her fast and hard after the one martini. All she wanted to do now was crawl in bed and sleep. She'd have to finish packing tomorrow. "What time do you head out?"

She had played this game before. When you were on the road as often as they both were, it wasn't uncommon to seek a bit of solace from the monotonous sterile hotel rooms. Drinks and sex were a way to wind down after the heady rush of performing. But after a few disastrous hook-ups, she had decided she needed a healthier way to cope.

She wasn't built for impersonal sex workouts. Besides, there were way too many complications in a close community like the classical musical world, especially with the men whose lack of a moral compass led to not sharing that they were married or only wanted one-night stands.

Instead, Emily adopted Stella, a French bulldog, as her traveling companion. Stella's antics and unconditional devotion helped Emily cope with her pre-performance anxiety and post-concert letdowns. After every performance, whether fantastic or not, Stella greeted Emily backstage with her enthusiastic yelps, her stout body swirling in circles, uncaring of the audience's reactions. Stella didn't care one lick about how Emily performed.

And after swearing off meaningless sex, Emily had violated her own rule for one man. Damn Nick Jenkins for remaining in her brain. She'd had seventy-two hours in a safe house with her bodyguard—sharing meals, watching action movies, comparing childhood stories about crazy brothers. She thought that it had meant something. She never imagined that the night they shared would be their only night together. Nick Jenkins, though he had a moral compass, only wanted a one-night stand.

"Did you call your driver?" Ben was texting.

"Charles should be outside. I told him two hours, knowing how difficult it would be for him to reach us at this hour on a Friday afternoon. Can he give you a lift or is your driver coming for you?" Emily searched the busy throughway for the town car. "I'm out by Berkeley, so it's easy to drop you off."

"I only use a driver on performance nights. I find the limo calls more attention. I like to go out incognito as much as I can. I use rideshares usually."

"I'm envious, but since I'm toting my cello and Stella, it makes it simpler. Part of my contract is to have a driver in every city." Emily didn't share that since her life had been threatened by North Korean spies and the Russian mob, her brother vetted her drivers, her hotels, and even her dog walkers.

Reeves, one of Emily's three older brothers and an intense computer geek, had gone all Rambo on her about the threat and still hadn't lightened up. His protective attitude had been reassuring at first, but it was time for Reeves to stop monitoring her life. She planned to have that conversation with her brother once she was in Seattle. There was no threat against her now, and she would never need a man like Nick Jenkins to guard her again.

Her life wasn't about spies, intrigue, and espionage. The biggest danger in her life was harsh critics or unreceptive audiences.

Emily dodged a group of tourists snapping pics of Ben with their phones. One whip-thin man wearing a baseball cap and sunglasses, despite the gray day, persisted, snapping endless pictures from his phone. "I don't have adoring fans who mob me like you do."

Ben was a household name, especially after he'd cut several songs with pop stars. He had crossed over into mainstream culture unlike Emily, who was known only in the classical music world.

"You have plenty of fans. You're on your way to becoming the next Jacqueline du Pré." She questioned whether Ben truly meant the compliment or was trolling, hoping to score. He was laying it on thick, comparing her to one of the most gifted cellists.

It had been a relief to forget Yuen Li's death for a while with Ben, but that's all it was. Just a break from returning to her rental to pack for Seattle and be spared from obsessing over the murder of Yuen.

"Jackie was sixteen when she captured the world." Not seeing the familiar town car, Emily searched in her purse for her phone to see if Charles had texted her that he was detained by the horrendous SF traffic. Digging her cell out of the crumpled Kleenexes, she tried to power up the black screen. Crap. Her phone was dead again. Between the shock of Yuen's death and jet lag, she had forgotten to charge her phone. Again. At least this time she had a good excuse for forgetting.

"And you were the ripe old age of what, *seventeen,* when you started performing?"

"I appreciate the comparison, but Jackie had a rare gift." Emily did identify with the famous performer and Jackie's incredible connection to the music. And like the earlier prodigy, Emily was considering taking a break from performing. The cost of translating music from your soul to an audience took a toll. Ben was right— she had started performing early; nine years later, she was tired.

She always swore after finishing a tour she would allow herself a break, but this time it was different. When she'd started touring, her goal had been to tour for fifteen years. Now she was reconsidering.

She wanted a life away from the continuous nomadic stress. Never away from music; just away from the touring—the endless hotel rooms, the demanding pressure and schedule, the constant change of cities and people.

"Oh, there he is." Emily pointed to the familiar black town car.

Ben pecked her on each cheek. "Thanks for the offer, but I think I'll walk to my hotel in Union Square. And thanks for sharing a drink." He took her elbow and guided her to the car double-parked on the busy street.

"I'm glad you were here today. My agent wanted to fly in from New York, but with the sudden…" Emily couldn't finish as grief took a chokehold again.

"The funeral was held quickly because of a family tradition coordinating the funeral with feng shui practices." Ben held the door for Emily to climb in.

"Charles. Thank you for—" Scooting into the car, Emily stopped midsentence. A muscle-bound man with a shaved head sat in the driver's seat.

"I'm sorry. I must have the wrong car." Emily slid to exit the car.

"Ms. Hewitt, I'm your driver. Charles took ill, and I'm filling in for him."

A shiver skittered across her bare arms. Emily couldn't place his Eastern European accent, despite her extensive travels through the region.

Ever since her life had been threatened four months ago, she was less trusting. After resisting the overprotective attitudes of her three older brothers for years, she was now more vigilant and less accepting of people. She could never go back into the bubble of her protected world. She now knew that evil people existed.

Ben leaned into the car. "Is there a problem?"

"I'm filling in for Ms. Hewitt's regular driver." The man stretched his bulky arm over the seat, a manacle tattoo encircling his wrist peeking out from beneath his suit jacket. "He didn't say anything about other passengers."

She didn't want to prejudge this man because his appearance and tats suggested Sing Sing or a biker's gang. But something was off. Why hadn't Charles texted her that he had a replacement? Duh. Because her phone was dead.

She was comfortable with Charles...not so much with this man. Charles had been driving for her for over a month during her music residency at UC Berkeley before she left for her Asia tour. "Ben, do you mind riding with me out to Berkeley?"

"I was instructed to pick up Ms. Hewitt. No one else. No other passengers."

"I'm not a passenger. I'm Ben Bellisiano." Ben's chest puffed up with his forceful, perfect articulation of a professional singer. Did Ben really believe this man would recognize a famous tenor?

The driver didn't move but continued his death stare toward Ben.

"I'm under contract with the company that I assume you and Charles both work for. You can call your boss, or I can if you'd prefer."

"It won't be necessary."

The menace in his voice made her skin crawl. She rubbed her arms trying to soothe the unsettling sensation.

"Where am I taking you, sir?"

"I'll accompany Miss Hewitt to Berkeley, and then you can return me to Union Square."

Emily squeezed Ben's hand and mouthed a silent "thank you." Something about the driver unsettled her. She didn't believe in premonitions, but going off alone with him would not have been a smart idea.

CHAPTER FIVE

Nick paid no attention to the No Parking sign as he pulled up in front of the bar. He stared at the giant, flashing red-neon letters on the yellow marquee.

Was the universe playing some kind of joke? The bar's name was "Fu Bar," an acronym used in the military for "Fucked Up Beyond All Recognition," which exactly matched his state of mind.

His resolution to avoid contact with Emily for months/years had suddenly imploded. He was FUBARed since he wasn't sure he had the ability to walk away from Emily a second time. He had fantasized about this reunion during many sleepless nights, but never in a dive in Chinatown called Fu Bar.

He pushed against the swinging door. Energy thrummed through his body in anticipation. The chance that Emily was in danger was slim and most likely fueled by Reeves's anxiety. And still, Nick wouldn't risk not being there for her.

Electronic music blasted in the dark, crowded space. Red lanterns were strung over the scarred wooden bar. Liquor was stacked on mirrored shelves with dangling sparkling lights. Under the cash register was an intricate black-and-gold canvas of pagodas and geishas.

He scanned the entire room, taking in the mix of tourists with their shopping bags and regulars with their heads bent over their drinks. His palms were sweaty, and he felt the uptick in his heart rate. In battle, he had complete control of his body, but the promise of seeing Emily had him in full adrenaline rush.

He walked to the rear of the seating area to check for back rooms. Nothing except a Chinese slot machine hanging on the wall between the restrooms and the kitchen.

He slid up to the bar and motioned to the bartender, a young woman with sleek black hair fashioned in a braid, her slim body encased in a tight red dress. She sauntered over with a smile as her heavily made-up eyes did a slow visual inspection, taking in his T-shirt and worn jeans.

"What can I get you?" Her voice was low and husky, a mismatch to her tiny frame.

Nick smiled and leaned over the bar in order to be able to hear over the din, giving her a taste of the Jenkins charm in the process. "I'm looking for my sister. She said to meet her here, but she's a no-show. Now she's not answering my texts. Classic for my kid sister."

He pulled out the only picture he had from Reeves. A beaming Emily held her cello on the stage at the Kennedy Center after her performance. He hadn't been able to delete it. He couldn't break the final tie to her.

"Was she here tonight?" Nick drew a twenty-dollar bill out of his wallet.

The bartender lifted the phone with her bright red nails and inspected the picture.

"Your sister?" She looked between the phone and Nick. Emily and he both had dark hair and dark eyes, but that was where the resemblance ended. Emily was beautiful and delicate like his mother's Sunday china. Nothing about Nick was delicate.

She raised her eyebrows. "Yeah, your sister was here, but you've got your work cut out for you. She was with Ben Bellisiano!" She fanned herself. "He's as hot as all his pictures… and what a voice. He gave me his autograph."

Emily was being comforted by a movie star or some famous dipshit. And he'd left his buddies to find her while she was— Nick shut down the image and instead, visualized wrapping his fingers around Reeves's throat. Except his vision clouded as he imagined Emily's pale neck and how he had found every sensitive spot on her responsive body.

"When did they leave?" He ignored the stab to his hard heart. Emily didn't owe him a damn thing.

And why shouldn't she be out with famous, hot men? Wasn't that the reason he had walked away? Wasn't it part of his damn plan?

"You just missed them. They left fifteen to twenty minutes ago."

"Thanks." Nick pushed the bill across the bar.

"She is one lucky woman to have two studs chasing her. I think you can give"—her black eyes raked over him again, pausing at his crotch—"Ben a run for his money."

Like he was going up against a megastar. Emily only deserved the best. And if she wanted a famous dude, he'd be happy for her…eventually.

"Thanks."

Nick's mood swung all over the place as he climbed into the truck. Jealousy was a bitch. He had no interest in any woman since his night with Emily, but she had moved on. He dialed Reeves, majorly pissed that he had rushed here using such a piddly-ass excuse to see Emily again.

"Hey, asshole," he growled into the phone. Reeves was lucky he was in Seattle.

"You found her? Thank God. Is she okay?"

"She wasn't abducted by aliens. She was at the bar with some famous dude named Ben Bellisiano and is probably going home with him right now." The idea of Emily sharing her perfect body and wild passion with another man was like pouring acid on an open wound. He death-gripped the steering wheel.

"Ben Bellisiano? I don't believe it," Reeves snapped. "She would never voluntarily go out with him."

"And why not?" Nick was Googling Ben Bellisiano as he listened to Reeves's rant.

"He's a major player. Emily can't stand men like him who use their position and fame to seduce women."

Nick stared at the bio of Bellisiano—a famous tenor and very good-looking, if you liked that metrosexual look and a weak chin.

"Emily is fine and out with a man." Nick almost choked on the words. "Get over it." He was saying the words more for himself. "Later."

Nick looked up at the glaring neon sign. Yeah. Tonight…a FUBAR.

"Wait. Nick, don't hang up. Just because she had a drink with a guy doesn't mean that she's in the clear. First, there was the murder of her tour manager and then men broke into her former studio. They could be planning on breaking into her apartment tonight. Why else disable the cameras? She could be in danger, and I can't warn her with her damn phone dead. You can't ignore all that's happened since she's been back in the States. Please, man, go to her apartment. I'll owe you."

Nick felt the heat of guilt creep up. He owed Reeves—enough to put himself through the torture of seeing Emily with another man. It was a stretch. But there was a reason his call name was "Duty."

And despite Reeves's irritating need to overshare tech details, the geek's judgment and skill were sound. Something was hinky about the murder—that someone close to Emily in the non-violent music industry had been murdered. The tour manager's death might be a random event, but until Nick knew for sure, he needed to make sure Emily was safe—despite the pain coming his way from being close to her.

"If you had a sister, you'd understand," Reeves pleaded. "Don't make me beg."

Oh, Nick understood Reeves's protective feelings toward Emily. Nick had them, and some other feelings for her, in spades.

"Emily is going to be so pissed at both of us for interrupting her night with the famous Ben."

Nick would never admit under the threat of death that he was a tiny bit glad for an excuse to interrupt Emily's night, hoping that seeing him would rekindle memories of their night together. And maybe seeing Emily involved with a douchebag might finally clear him of his feelings that what they shared was special—a big maybe.

He continued, "I won't make you beg. But you'll have to handle Emily when she goes ballistic." Emily definitely had the artistic temperament.

Reeves chuckled. "I can handle my sister."

Spoken like a stupid man. Nick might not have a sister, but he never underestimated the strength of women. His mother had taught him that lesson very early when his father had passed. Under all that soft warmness, Emily had the discipline and drive to become a successful musician. Reeves only saw Emily as his little sister and not the powerful woman she had become.

"This is on your head, man."

"Just call me when you're with her, and I'll take the heat."

Nick made a U-turn and headed to Berkeley, refusing to acknowledge the warm sensation in his chest at the thought of seeing Emily again…with another man. Proof that he was pathetic. He could hear his buddies laughing their asses off if they ever got wind of tonight.

Seeing her apartment building, Emily couldn't wait to escape the tense silence of the town car. The eight-mile drive to Berkeley felt like eighty. The martini had been a short-lived panacea to the emotionally wrenching funeral. Sliding out of the car, she limped to the front door, unable to hide the ache in her feet from wearing four-inch Jimmy Choos. She willed herself to smile as she waved at Ben waiting at the car. Only a few more steps to pick up Stella before she could crash.

She glanced up at the camera that Nick had installed above the entrance to her apartment building, ensuring that she had the latest in security protection after the threat. She was not a paranoid person in the least, but in the past few days, Emily couldn't shake the eerie sensation that someone was watching her. Not necessarily paranoia since someone she cared about had been senselessly murdered. She wrapped her pashmina around her shoulders with a sudden shiver. She'd be glad to escape damp and chilly San Francisco.

She entered the electronic passcode to open the door, then waved to Ben that she was safely in the building. She was appreciative that Ben had escorted her home. Had she not been with Ben, she would never have gotten into the town car without confirming with Charles that the spooky man was Charles's replacement. It wasn't the driver's appearance but the sinister energy radiating off him that triggered alarms. Despite her brothers' opinion, she wasn't an idiot.

She had traveled all over the world from an early age without an incident. Her brothers considered her a fragile prodigy who had to be protected at all times. Just because she wasn't an A-to-B linear thinker and she didn't see danger in every corner didn't mean that she wasn't a highly functional person. Her mother, a brilliant mathematician, was the only family member supportive of Emily's "artistic idiosyncrasies."

She didn't plan to share her concerns about tonight's driver with Reeves or her feelings about being followed. Knowing how high-handed and overbearing Reeves was, she might end up being guarded by Nick Jenkins again. She hated thinking about the man. Like never-ending spam in her email, she had deleted from her life, he kept reappearing. She didn't need another domineering man in her life. She had three brothers, who were more than enough to handle.

Emily climbed up the stairs to the second-floor apartments. Douglas and Richard were babysitting Stella tonight. With the last-minute timing of the funeral, Emily had scrambled to find a spot for Stella.

Knocking on their door, she heard Stella's welcoming yelp. How did Stella know it was her?

Richard, Douglas's partner, opened the door. Despite barely knowing either man—they'd moved in while she was on tour—she and Stella had immediately bonded with the two very striking men.

Emily had been desperate when she asked them to take care of Stella to attend the funeral. The men had been gracious in helping her.

Richard pulled her into his arms, wrapping her in a hug while Stella danced at her feet. "Was it horrible? You poor thing!"

Tears burned her eyes. She had held it together, but Richard's genuine concern coupled with pure exhaustion made her shaky on her feet. She wanted to be held and comforted. She didn't want to be alone tonight.

CHAPTER SIX

Nick pulled the truck in front of Emily's apartment. He scanned the neighborhood. A black sedan was parked on the opposite side of the street, giving the male driver a perfect view of the apartment building's entrance. By the looks of it, the car was a Taurus, the choice of law enforcement agencies. Did the police suspect Emily in her friend's murder? She had been the last one to speak with him. He needed to read that damn report. Without facts, he was running blind. He couldn't ignore all the possibilities until Reeves had the information.

Nick climbed out of the truck, deciding whether to approach the car to see the reaction of the driver to identify whether they were with law enforcement. If the man was still out here when Nick left, he would confront him. Nick walked to the front door, inspecting the camera. No indication that it had been tampered with.

He punched the password into the electronic keypad and entered the building. The brick building had the same musty smell he remembered but was well-maintained. He climbed the stairwell to Emily's second-floor apartment, playing every scenario in his mind. What if Ben and Emily were in the bedroom? Undressed. He shut down the idea. He would deliver Reeves's message, he'd get answers to reassure himself about her safety, and then he'd get the hell out of there.

His heart was ratcheting all over the place. This wasn't part of his plan. He needed to avoid her for a few more months/years. Get her out of his system. Be able to think of her like the sister of a friend. His plans for the future was to eventually see her as nothing but a distant stranger. The one thing he learned from all the losses he endured over the years was that time helped everything. But he wasn't going to get the bloody time and distance from her anytime soon.

He reached the top step. And his eyes couldn't take in the sight. Emily was in the arms of a tall blond dude in the hallway across from her apartment. Not Ben, the famous singer. Where was her date?

By the way her head rested against the guy's muscular chest, they were more than friends. Red flashing lights exploded in front of Nick's eyes. His finely tuned control over his body and his delusion that he was over Emily shattered into a primitive and possessive rage.

"What the hell?"

Nick charged down the hallway as his body stiffened, and every sinew prepared for battle. Stella raced toward him, yelping with joy. Her wheelbarrow body almost tripped over her stubby, fast-moving legs.

Emily twisted and pulled out of the surfer's arms. "Nick?"

The tall blond who still had his hands on Emily had the stones to smile at Nick. Was he kidding? Didn't this dude read male-speak? He was about to get his ass kicked.

Stella jumped on Nick's leg, yelping in excitement. Nick had to greet the dog or she would escalate into a dirge-like howl. He lifted Stella into his arms. The little sausage dog's attempts to lick his face and uncontrollable wiggling body overpowered his kill-and-maim mode.

Patting Stella's head helped Nick pull his shit together. What was he doing, going all caveman? He couldn't claim any rights to Emily.

Emily brushed her long, silky hair away from her face, her espresso colored eyes searching his. She faltered backward away from the guy and pressed her hand to her chest. "My God, has something happened to Reeves?"

The panic that flashed across her face deflated Nick's reaction to another man touching her. "No, honey. Reeves is fine."

"I don't understand."

"Reeves sent me. Your phone is dead, and he was worried." The moment when Nick might have been able to pull her into his arms passed in an instant as her forehead wrinkled into displeasure and her black eyes narrowed.

"You made the trek from Seattle to check on me because my phone is dead?"

Nick raised his hand but stopped himself before touching her. "Let me explain."

She backed away and crossed her arms. "And what is Reeves worried about this time?"

He tried to ignore the way her arms pushed her cleavage forward in the low-cut, short, black dress. The blood rushed from his brain. He wanted to cover her in the shawl draped over her arm and whisk her away from the man watching with appreciative eyes.

"Can we discuss this in private?" Nick nodded toward surfer dude, who was engrossed in the drama, not trying to hide in the least his interest in the byplay.

"By the way, I'm Richard."

A second tall, blond man joined.

"I'm Douglas, Richard's partner. We've been dog sitting Stella. Look at that hussy. She had me believing I was the only man in her life."

Stella was licking Nick's face.

Nick's neck flushed with embarrassment. He had just made a complete ass of himself. He really might be losing it as his brothers suggested. He always was a steady kind of guy. But recently, he had more mood swings than a pregnant woman. He offered his hand to Richard, whom he had been on the verge of taking down. "I'm Nick Jenkins. Stella and I go way back."

Emily snorted.

Douglas offered his hand. "Nice to meet you, Nick."

Emily leaned forward and lifted Stella out of Nick's arms, avoiding any physical contact with him.

"Thanks for delivering Reeves's message. I'll make sure to charge my phone." She rubbed Stella's ears and averted her gaze.

"I'm not here to tell you to charge your phone. I need to talk with you in private. This is important."

Emily turned on her high heels, her dress tight around her round ass as she crossed the hall. This woman had curves, the kind of curves that could make a man insane. She had worn that dress for that bloody singer.

"Reeves can tell me tomorrow whatever was so important to send you scurrying here."

"Scurrying?" Nick was usually slow to erupt, but this woman had the affront to imply he, a Spec Force operator, a US Marine captain, was an errand boy. Jealousy and frustration fomented to breaking point, fueled by the idea of another man peeling that little dress off her.

Emily shifted Stella to her hip to open her door.

"I'll only take five minutes. I won't interrupt your night with the legendary Ben Bellisiano."

Emily pivoted and stomped on her way-too-high heels to stand close. Her breasts quivered in shock. "OMG, you've been stalking me. It's you who's been following me. It wasn't my imagination."

All his jealousy and possessiveness vanished. "Someone has been following you? Since when?"

"It wasn't you?"

Hearing the worry in her voice, Nick wanted to soothe her but knew she wasn't open to anything from Nick Jenkins when she had Ben Bellisiano waiting for her.

"We need to talk. You need to tell me what the hell is going on."

"I don't need to tell you anything. I'm fine. It's been a rough three days, but I'll be in Seattle tomorrow and this will all be behind me."

He leaned around her and entered the code, opening the door to allow Emily and Stella to enter.

Of course, she didn't follow his lead but crossed the hallway where Richard and Douglas waited. "Thanks again, guys, for taking care of Stella."

"We're sorry about your friend, and we wish you weren't leaving." Douglas hugged her firmly.

Emily swallowed hard. "I'm sorry too. Remember, if you make it to New York, call me."

She swept by Nick, who held the door open. And he swallowed as her scent rose off her warm body as she went by him without touching.

CHAPTER SEVEN

Nick followed Emily and Stella into the apartment. He tried to not track the sway of Emily's sweet backside. The high heels thrust her body forward, emphasizing the hypnotic motion. It took all his military training to look away. He exhaled slowly and readied himself to meet Bellisiano and act like a graduate of the Naval Academy—the disciplined marine that he was. He could control his urges and not act like a crazy jealous asshat.

He refused to accept that Emily was serious about this star after what Reeves said.

God, he hoped Bellisiano hadn't undressed while Emily was retrieving Stella. Naked or not, Bellisiano was going to have to deal with Nick Jenkins. He didn't give a shit if he was interrupting their hookup, because Nick wasn't leaving until he had answers. The game had changed with her admission that she had been followed. The Taurus sedan he'd spotted was now front and center on Nick's radar.

No one, including lover boy, would deter him from protecting Emily. He was trained to serve and protect, unlike Bellisiano, who was trained to sing high notes.

Emily bent over to release Stella, sending the dress riding up her toned thighs. His heart pounded against his chest like a drum in the navy's marching band. Having Emily this close and not being able to touch her was worse than any hellhole he'd endured.

Watching Emily's movements was like watching a sensual

ballet. It took a minute for Nick to realize that Bellisiano wasn't in the small apartment. Nick could see into the bedroom with the door wide open, and it was empty. Emily hadn't invited Bellisiano inside her place. And suddenly Nick felt like a young boy on Christmas morning.

"It's been crazy." Emily scooped up clothing that was scattered on the coffee table. "Believe it or not, this is organized." The couch and chairs were covered with clothes. The only clear space was the corner near the window where her cello sat next to a music stand piled with sheets of music.

The sight of her cello brought back the haunting sounds burned in his brain and heart. In the cramped space of their Sausalito safe house, Emily had practiced daily in the living room for her upcoming tour. His taste in music was hard rock—angry, aggressive, and loud.

Nick was unprepared and forever changed by Emily's ethereal beauty combined with the music—the emotional, heartrending melodies wrought by the delicacy of her fingers and bow. He had no reference to explain how this woman communicated tenderness and splendor to his soul, a soul he didn't recognize or acknowledge.

"I sent most of my clothes home to New York but haven't had time today…with the"—she swallowed hard—"to pack for Seattle."

Emily's nervous chatter helped Nick. She was as off-kilter as he was. She avoided looking at him. She wasn't in any better control of the flammable combustion and memories flaring between them.

"You've had a lot to deal with. And a lot of clothes to drag around." He tried to lighten the mood. Knowing how much she valued her independence away from her three brothers, she wouldn't want to appear vulnerable. Especially in front of him.

Emily turned to face him. There was an air of fragility around her that he had never seen. She was pale, her bloodshot eyes offset by dark circles. He wanted to pull her into his arms and spare her from all the trauma. She wouldn't allow him to be a comfort.

"When you're a soldier, you don't have to worry." Nick smiled. "No piles of clothes or decisions on what to pack."

"I needed to crash like two hours ago. The jet lag has caught up with me. Can you please deliver the message from Reeves and then go away?"

Nick faltered at the sight of the red thong and matching bra flung over the arm of the chair. *Stab me in the eye with a fork.* Searing heat surged through him. Burned in his brain was the memory of luscious Emily wearing the tiny thong and bra and how he had slowly peeled away the sexy items. All his blood flow went south.

His gasp alerted Emily to look at him. Their gazes locked. He couldn't hide the possessiveness and need roaring through him. Electric shocks arced between them before Emily dropped her eyes and fidgeted with the gold locket which hung on a chain around her neck.

He cleared his throat, trying to regain his control. "Why didn't you call me or Reeves when your tour manager was murdered? We could have helped."

Her head snapped back as if she had been struck. "You expected me to call you?"

Her honest bewilderment hurt in a way he hadn't expected.

"I told you I'd always have your back."

"Is that a joke?" Emily shook her head and then busied herself stacking the clothing from the couch.

"Tell me what happened with your manager."

"No." She straightened and frowned. "There is nothing for us to discuss."

"We have plenty to discuss."

Emily rolled her eyes and marched to the bedroom. "Fine, you discuss. I'm going to sleep and pray that when I wake up, you'll be gone."

"Not happening. I will wait for you right here." Nick pushed a pile of dresses to one side of the couch and sat, avoiding the chair with her kill-a-man lingerie. If he got close to the silky stuff, he might lose his cool. He was hanging by a thread, sensations and needs that he had shut down for four long months whirring through him.

Stella jumped into his lap, saving him again from making a complete jerk out of himself by admitting that he had hoped every day that she would call him. And how happy he was tonight for an excuse to be with her again. "Do you want me to feed Stella?"

Stella yelped at Nick's question.

He could hear Emily's light laugh, the warm sound soothing the beast he was keeping at bay. "That's a yes."

The beast twitched against his zipper with the vision of Emily squirming out of the tight dress and standing in a thong and bra not more than ten feet away from him.

Stella yipped again. "You're hungry?" Nick rubbed along Stella's soft upright ears and then under her double chin. "You're always hungry."

Stella jumped off the couch and ran to a tin where her kibble was stored.

Nick poured warm water over her food, enjoying the intimate routine as if he were a part of Emily's and Stella's life, while Stella danced in circles.

He lowered the monogrammed bowl to the matching monogrammed mat on the floor. Stella, like her owner, was very stylish. In any other woman, Nick would have thought it was an affectation, but with Emily, he considered her devotion endearing.

He washed his hands in the kitchen sink before returning to the living room where Emily waited. She had changed into yoga pants and a baggy T-shirt without a bra—not that he should be noticing. But he was a male. And males noticed important details.

The thick ebony hair that he remembered across his chest was pulled up into a high ponytail. The memory of her in the same outfit in the safe house knocked him off-center. This stunning woman had no idea how she had him twisted in knots.

Emily sat in the chair with the hanging red bra and thong. She folded the burn-a-hole-in-his-retina items before placing them on her lap. Obviously, Emily wasn't plagued like he was by flashes of heat and lust.

"I'll explain, and then you have to promise me you'll go away so I can sleep."

"I can't promise until I hear everything." Since she was willing to talk with him, Nick decided not to share that he wasn't leaving her until she was safely in Seattle.

"Fine. But I hope that oath you took as a US Marine will mean that you'll act honorably in this at least."

Nick flinched at her unexpected attack. Emily thought he was like every loser who made promises during sex and then disappeared the next day. In his head, he had done the honorable thing by disappearing. How could he explain to Emily of the welcoming smiles, believer of goodness and beauty in the world, that his life had led him to cynicism and darkness?

"Your uninvited appearance is the reason I didn't tell Reeves. How did he find out anyway? Izzy would never have ratted me out."

Nick dropped to the couch to face Emily. "Don't be tough on Reeves. There is more that you need to hear. The cameras I installed at your studio and here at the apartment have been disabled."

Emily yawned widely then stretched her neck, showing no visible reaction to the news. Jet lag was unpredictable, but when it hit, you just bottomed out. Traveling for Uncle Sam, he understood the sudden crash from changing time zones. Of course, he was trained to override his body's circadian rhythm.

"But I moved out of the studio over four months ago, and I'm leaving here tomorrow. What difference could it possibly make?"

Nick hesitated to tell her about the break-in and his suspicion that she was a target for some reason. He didn't want to bring her any more bad news, but she deserved the facts. And despite his tendency not to divulge, the only way that he'd get her cooperation was to be straight with her.

"The studio was broken into tonight. That both cameras were disabled might mean that your apartment would be next. Reeves tried to call you when he learned of the break-in, but your phone was dead. He called Izzy."

"And when he found out about Yuen Li, he called you."

"He knew I was in San Francisco visiting my buddies, so yeah...he called me." The words didn't convey any of the schizophrenic swing of emotions he had lived through in the past two hours. Or the rightness and comfort he felt just being near her. The memories pouring over him reminded him how much he liked her, the contentment he felt spending time with her.

Emily crossed her legs into a yoga position, and another familiar intimacy washed over him. "Thank you for interrupting your visit with your friends. If you lend me your phone, I can reassure Reeves that I'm fine and, as you can see, no one has broken into my apartment. Despite it looking like it has been ransacked." There was a gleaming twinkle that lit up her big, round eyes. The way her upper lip curved into slight amusement warmed Nick's ice-encased feelings.

"And I'm leaving here in less than"—she looked at her watch and moaned—"in less than six hours, so you can get back to your friends."

Nick wanted to smile. He wasn't so easily dismissed. "Tell me more about why you thought someone was following you."

She yawned again and leaned her head against the chair and closed her eyes. "It wasn't anything specific, just a feeling. I felt like someone was watching me, but I never saw anyone, and no one approached me. I decided it was the shock about Yuen Li."

"You should always trust your gut. Instincts are really important. Did you notice anyone who made you feel uncomfortable?"

"No." She almost looked like she was asleep, then she sat straight up. "You think the disabled cameras are related to Yuen Li's death? That's the reason you're here?"

"Not that I know of yet...but there is a possibility."

"What aren't you telling me? Just give it to me. I'm way too tired to play games with you."

"I've told you everything I know. Being the last person to speak to your manager before he was killed and then having the studio break-in could be a coincidence. But my job doesn't allow me to ignore coincidences. Is there anything else? Anything unusual that has happened since you returned to the States?"

"Besides having a dear friend murdered?" She turned her head to gaze out the window.

"I'm sorry. And I wish you had called me for support. I've had experience losing good friends." He wasn't sure why he just shared something he never discussed. His losses were all kept in a steel cage in an area of his mind that he never planned to allow out. You couldn't do your job if you examined too closely or felt too much.

Emily stared out the window.

"When did you start to feel like someone was following you?"

She unfolded her legs and turned toward him. "The past three days are all a blur… I guess when I left the police station. I kept turning around, expecting to see someone, but no one was there. And, at the time, I thought talking about my friend's murder with the police was making me paranoid."

"You didn't have anyone with you when you went to the station?"

She shook her head. "Stella. And Charles drove me."

Nick didn't like the idea that Emily had been unprotected and alone since the murder. His trusted instincts were delivering karate kicks to his chest.

"There *was* something strange." She rubbed her eyes with both fists like a sleepy child. "Charles had a substitute driver today. Charles has never missed driving me while I've been here. And the substitute…"

Nick straightened in the chair with the sudden tension in Emily's voice.

"I didn't want to be judgmental, but he gave off a scary vibe. He looked like he took steroids and he had a manacle tat around his wrist. That's what men in Eastern Europe have if they've gone to prison."

"You got in the car with his guy?"

"God, you are just like my brothers. As if I don't know how to take care of myself!"

"I know how capable you are. And I've never judged your ability. You just came from a funeral, so it would be understandable if you let down your guard when you've been through such a hellish experience."

Emily raised one perfect eyebrow as she slowly inspected his face. He guessed she was taking a read on his bullshit meter. She started to answer, but Stella came barreling into the living room and jumped on Emily's lap. The dog smiled up at Emily as if knowing Emily needed support. "I did get in the car because Ben was with me. But you already know that since you and Reeves were tracking me."

"Oh, the renowned Ben." He couldn't hide the jealous snideness in his voice. "As if he could fight off an abduction."

"Yes, the famous Ben, who made sure that I was safely delivered to my front door. And believe it or not, I wouldn't have gotten into the car if Ben wasn't with me."

"If he's such a great protector"—Nick felt the throb in his forehead—"then why isn't Ben here now?"

"What?"

Trying not to reveal how unsettled he felt, he took out his phone. "I'm calling Reeves to run a check on your driver. Reeves would have vetted the car service. We need to know that Charles's substitute was legit."

"This all sounds too fantastical. Losing Yuen Li is hard enough, but to think… It's just too much. I need to sleep before I process all this. I'm in a total brain fog right now."

"We'll have Reeves check out the new driver. Then we can decide."

"This is insane. The police believe Yuen Li was killed for his wallet, expensive watch, and new iPhone."

"And that truly may be. You don't have to do anything right now. Go ahead and crash. I'm staying here tonight. Once Reeves gets back to me, we can decide our next step."

"You're staying here?" She bolted out of the chair with Stella in her arms. "Don't I have a say in who's staying at my place?"

He jumped off the couch and moved to invade her space. "Until you get to Seattle, I'll be staying close. I'm not taking any chances with your safety."

Emily didn't flinch or step back as he towered over her, trying to intimidate her with his size. Hard-ass soldiers retreated from his power play, but not Emily.

"I'm too tired to fight about this tonight. I don't have the energy. And since you are just like my brothers, I know that you'll do what you want despite how I feel. I guess I should thank you for being concerned." She walked to the bedroom, keeping her back to him. "Thank you for your help. The piles of clothes have been sorted. Don't mess them up."

She slammed the door shut.

CHAPTER EIGHT

Emily was having the best dream. Nick whispered to her, his musky male scent and warmth enveloping her in a cocoon of safety. She didn't want this dream to end, but she already knew he would leave her alone and afraid.

"Emily. Wake up, honey."

She moaned at the sound of his melodic bass voice— the rich and flawless tone resonated in his highly developed chest muscles.

"Emily."

She lingered in the pleasure. "Basso profundo. With deep tessitura."

"Honey, you're dreaming about your music. Wake up."

She reached for him, rubbing her hand along his rough stubble. It felt exactly as she remembered. "This dream feels so real. Kiss me, Nick. I want to feel your lips on mine."

She felt his soft lips brush across hers. She opened her mouth, wanting to taste him. She'd never forget his tender and demanding kisses. "Please, Nick."

"Emily, you need to wake up." He used the rumbly sexy voice she liked.

Why was he insisting she wake when she was happy? She felt a rough hand on her arm. She opened her eyes, trying to orient herself. What tour…What hotel was this? Stella began licking Emily's face.

"We need to get going."

What was wrong? Nick's voice had gone from soft to fortissimo loud.

"Emily, wake up."

"Nick?" Her dream had conjured the real Nick.

"Yes. It's Nick." Now he sounded irritated. What had she done?

She hovered between asleep and awake, not sure if the kiss was real. She wanted to drift back to sleep where she and Nick were in bed together.

"Emily, we're late." His voice wasn't that of a tender lover. She definitely was awake.

"For my flight?" She never missed her flights. Well, almost never. She rolled on to her back, trying to care about on-time boarding. But until she had her coffee, she couldn't generate anxiety about her flight. If she had a performance, that was one thing. Otherwise, there was always another flight.

"You need to get dressed now."

She tugged on the blanket, trying to dislodge Stella's weight to hide her revealing camisole. His closeness was too intimate… bringing back too many memories of their one night together. One long, intense, very personal night. The scent of Nick flooded her mind. Opened the memories she had worked hard to repress into a tiny part of her brain never to be accessed again.

"Get moving." Now she found no pleasure in his voice. It was rough and mimicked the tone and pitch he probably used to command the men under him. But he wasn't her commanding officer, and she wasn't budging until she was good and ready. Nick was trying to take over her life before she had her coffee. She could catch the next flight.

Jet lag had smacked her last night, leaving her without the energy to resist Reeves or Nick's plans. But after sleeping, she was ready to take on the domineering man who acted like he had the right to waltz in and take over her life and bring back all the pain.

"It's not safe. You're in danger. We need to move."

Emily bolted upright. "What?"

"I'm sorry, Emily. Your driver's body was found."

She could barely get a breath out. "Charles? Dead?"

"I know this is a shock. But I need you to get up and get dressed. We need to leave. Now!"

Her heart raced into triplets like a baroque sonata. She lifted Stella from the blanket to free herself and swung her legs to the floor. Forget the coffee. Fear sped through her like a major caffeine fix. "But who would kill Charles?"

"I don't know. We can talk about this once we're out of here. Get dressed while I pack up Stella."

"But I have to pack my clothes." The words went directly from her racing brain out her mouth. She realized how ridiculous it was to think about her clothes, but she needed to cling to something to make sense of her spinning-out-of-control world.

She and Nick had rehearsed what she should do if she had to evacuate the safe house in Sausalito, but she never had to. The criminals had been captured before they could act on the threat against her and Stella. This was the real event. Her heart sped into a frantic pace that rivaled Rimsky-Korsakov's "Flight of the Bumblebees."

With the adrenaline surging through her body, she scurried to the living room to gather jeans and a sweater. "Where are we going?"

"To the Oakland airport."

Nick's intense focus and clipped answers telegraphed the seriousness of the danger.

"One of Dean's jets is en route to pick us up."

"Okay…but… I can't leave my cello."

"Of course."

Thank God, he didn't fight her on the cello. She wasn't leaving her only link to Yuen Li. He had arranged to have the priceless cello given to her. She had sent her two other cellos back to New York.

Emily hurried. She stuffed underwear and a couple of tops and yoga pants into her bag. She was glad to focus on a mundane task because she didn't want to think about Charles or his three children and the stories that he shared about them. And she didn't want to imagine why anyone would kill the decent and upright man she considered a friend. The two men she had been closest to during her West Coast stay were dead. Shock and grief hovered, ready to consume her. She grabbed her ankle boots and rushed into the living room. This was not the time to dwell on the pain.

Nick had packed her cello into its case.

"I don't understand any of this. Both men dead? Why?" Emily stuffed the sheets with her handwritten music notes and her computer into the bag and then slipped on her boots.

"We'll use the back stairs. You carry Stella. I'll take everything else."

Emily lifted a subdued Stella, who wasn't yipping or dancing, seeming to have picked up on the tension.

Nick used the straps on her travel cello case to slip it on like a backpack. He swung her carry bag over his left arm, then drew a gun from the back of his blue jeans.

Emily gasped. The reality was right there in the lethal weapon. No denying the danger when faced with Nick's intense focus, gun in hand, his body tight, his eyes shuttered.

He lifted her chin and gazed into her eyes. "Once I get you out of here, I'm going to deliver on the kiss you asked for."

Emily's shock must have registered on her face judging by Nick's sudden grin. How absolutely mortifying. Nothing like blowing her "I don't care" mojo. And distracting her from the danger.

"Follow me." Nick slowly opened the door to the back stairwell, giving Emily a signal to follow. Silently, she and Stella proceeded. Her heart raced in vivacissimo tempo, making her lightheaded.

Focused on Nick, she ignored the pulsating fear. His tension and awareness forced her into the same mode. This was no drill. This was as real as Yuen Li's casket.

After descending the stairwell, he slowly opened the outside door. The stiff tension radiating off his body surrounded Emily, who had Stella clenched in a steely grip.

"It's okay, girl," Emily whispered, trying to soothe her dog, not wanting Stella to bark in anticipation of going outside. Her voice was high pitched and sounded strange to her ears.

Nick walked to the side of the building and made the same tense move where he led with his gun, ready to confront anyone who waited to attack them.

Emily was barely breathing by the time they reached the street. Nick's combat maneuvers had pushed her close to panic. Emily took a deep breath, unconsciously using her discipline as a musician to focus on keeping a cool head and following Nick's lead. Her charge was to remain calm and follow directions. Confronting dangerous people with guns wasn't in her wheelhouse. Thank God.

Her brothers had tried to force her to learn how to use a firearm, but she had been adamant that she had no desire to handle a gun. At this moment, she was reconsidering.

At least she had taken self-defense classes. After the threat against her life, Emily had returned to Berkeley and signed up for private lessons. She would never again feel helpless like she had when the North Koreans had planned to kill her and Stella.

Emily followed Nick down the narrow alley between the two apartment buildings, past the recycle and garbage bins, reaching the corner of the building. Nick scanned the street in both directions from his hidden position.

"Stay here until I can check out the truck." He tucked his gun into his jeans under the cello case. Would he be able to grab the gun if he needed it? Was she risking his life by not leaving her cello? Then she realized Nick would've forced her to leave it if it compromised her safety. Nick would have no qualms about sacrificing the musical instrument. Which was a big mark against him. But he had put up no fuss so far. All part of the paradox that was Nick Jenkins.

"Once I know the truck is safe—"

Why wouldn't the truck be safe? A terrible thought flashed through Emily's mind. She couldn't stop her breath from coming in pants. She sounded like Stella with her raspy breath, but she couldn't catch her breath.

"Safe like…from a bomb?" Emily gulped.

"Most likely tracking devices." His gaze roved the street, never stopping.

Why did a tracking device sound good and normal?

"I'll open the passenger door, and then you and Stella walk toward the truck like normal. Can you do that? If we're being watched, we don't want to alert them that we're on to them."

"I'm a performer. I can act nonchalant. I project calm to an audience of thousands." At least she had one talent to contribute to this nightmare.

"That's my girl." Nick grinned, and a warmth spread through her tight chest. Two smiles from Nick and she was acting like a fangirl. She remembered how he'd started his bodyguarding duty all business four months ago, but how easily he'd laughed and smiled and the way the darkness left his eyes during their last day together.

"And if anything happens, you run."

And poof…her millisecond of happiness vanished.

"I don't want anything to happen to you."

"Don't worry, I can take care of myself."

Right. As if he could stop speeding bullets. Then again, if it hit his heart, maybe he could repel them.

CHAPTER NINE

To remain still and watch Nick slowly ramble down the sidewalk toward the red truck was excruciating. Her heartbeat sprinted, and her breath came in short pants. She wanted to run after him, shout to stop him, do something, do anything more than wait alone in the alley.

He leaned the cello against the driver's door. He scanned the street both ways, then bent to look under his truck. Walking to the front, he kicked both front tires before running his hand along the bumpers. He continued to feel and inspect until he circled back and opened the driver's door.

Nick's every movement had Emily's heart reverberating against her chest like the percussion section in the gargantuan Gothic symphony.

He carefully placed her cello in the trunk, started the truck, and then circled around the front to open the passenger door, keeping Emily in view.

Sweat dripped down her back while chills ran along her arms. She exhaled deeply, then walked out from the alley. Her knees and hands trembled as she cooed nonsense to Stella. She was trying to act normal as she searched the block. No one. It was too early for university students to be out. She placed Stella in the truck and then climbed into the high cab's front seat.

Nick closed Emily's door then walked to the front of the truck, his eyes repeatedly scanning the street before he got in. "You did good, honey."

Nick placed his gun on his lap, pointed toward the door, then handed her his phone. At the sight of the weapon, any safety she felt from being in the truck vanished. Her heart was racing like a high-speed metronome.

"Hit Tanner in my contacts and put him on speaker."

"Your team is helping?" She should feel bad for involving his marine buddies, but she couldn't muster anything but relief. She'd met them a few months ago. His team were all superheroes and highly competent marines. All muscle, arrogant and confident like Nick. No matter how she felt about Nick, she didn't want him to be in danger. His men would protect him too.

"En route?" Tanner's deep voice, lower and rougher than Nick's, came through loud and clear in the truck's cab.

"No problems. The black sedan is gone."

"What black sedan?" Emily squeaked in a high C range.

"Hey, Emily, how are you holding up? Bet you were surprised to see Nick again."

Did she hear amusement in his voice? Of course, the men knew how close Nick and she had gotten in Sausalito. It was hard to hide the shared night when the men rotated watching outside the house and there were cameras installed inside.

Did they also know that Nick had ghosted her? Probably standard behavior for all the alpha males who had women drooling over them. She should know since her brothers were still single, except for Reeves, who had a girlfriend.

"I didn't think I'd be needing your help again." She was having an out-of-body experience keeping up the pretense of a chat with an old acquaintance while danger swirled around her.

"We've got your back, sweetheart."

"She's not your sweetheart," Nick said.

Tanner's belly laugh almost brought a smile to Emily's face. She could see the gigantic man with fiery red hair and piercing green eyes. He was like a big teddy bear who loved to joke, except for the fact that he was seven feet of solid muscle.

"We'll reach the Twenty-Four and Tunnel Road in less than ten minutes," Nick said.

Emily stared at Nick's profile. His eyes shifted constantly—from the rear window, to the side windows, to the road ahead. And her heart whacking against her ribs was back.

"Roger that. We'll wait for you at the Twenty-Four intersection. And we'll stay behind to see what tails you have. I'll keep the line open."

"I don't see anyone yet. The black sedan might catch up."

Although Nick and the men were calm and businesslike, Emily wasn't reassured. Not when Nick kept his constant vigilance and a lethal weapon on his lap.

"Our ETA is less than five minutes. Carter and I are in my SUV, but Logan's truck has been modified and should handle whatever comes your way."

"Logan said not to mess up his truck or he'll kick your ass." Emily recognized Carter's baritone.

"Emily is on the line. Watch your language, asswipe," Tanner said.

"You just called me asswipe. What's the difference between asswipe and asshole?"

"Carter, no worries. I've heard everything from my older brothers." Emily was used to smack talk with her brothers, but not when everyone's lives were at risk. This whole situation was unreal.

"You sure know how to bring some excitement to our old team and to our sad-sack commander. None of us have had this much fun since Sausalito."

"Shut the fuck up, Carter." Tanner forgot his ban on swearing. "This isn't fun for her."

"Yeah, shut the fuck up, Carter," Nick boomed.

"I'm sorry that I've involved you in this mess. But I'll soon be out of your hair." She didn't know how to banter in life-or-death situations.

"We like being in your hair. Oh, shit, that didn't come out the way it should have. My apologies, Emily."

"Nick is going to kill you, Carter."

Emily giggled, a definite sign that she was stressed and didn't belong in their macho world.

Nick turned sharply at the sound of her giggle. "You holding up?"

"I'm fine." Sure, if being on the run from criminals can be considered "fine."

"I just picked up the black sedan from Derby Street. He's two cars behind me," Nick said.

"We're being followed?" There was her high-pitched squeak again. Emily's pulse skipped a beat or two. The men had bantered to distract her, help her forget she wasn't a super soldier ready to take on the bad guys.

Nick squeezed her knee. "We've got this covered. Don't worry."

"Are you kidding?" Was he that dense?

"What Duty means, Emily, is that we were expecting you to be followed. We're here to take care of whoever follows you. Carter and I can handle any threat."

Emily had forgotten Nick's call sign. Too bad Nick didn't feel that "duty" included explaining why he disappeared.

"Who is in the black sedan?" She felt out of control and wanted to know everything that was happening. It was the way she conquered new music. She focused on the details, not giving in to being overwhelmed with the giant task of learning the entire piece. One section at a time. If she thought about Yuen Li and Charles being murdered by the men following them, she'd freak.

"The Ford Taurus was parked in front of the apartment building when I arrived last night. It could have been a random occurrence, but since the car and driver are behind us, it obviously wasn't." Nick shrugged.

"The man who killed Charles and Yuen Li is behind us?" Emily tried to lessen the fear in her voice. Maybe she didn't want details. There was something lovely about remaining ignorant—like not having the sensation that someone Tanner's size was sitting on your chest.

Nick twisted to look at her. "Unlikely. That make and model is usually used in law enforcement. Most likely San Francisco police are watching you because of your tie to Yuen Li."

"I'm a suspect? Of all the outrageous bullshit. The police think I might be responsible for killing Yuen Li?" Emily couldn't keep up with the surprises as her stomach twisted into tight knots. "But what about Charles? They think I killed him too? Cellist on a rampage? They must be desperate."

"You are on their radar because you were the last one to talk with Yuen Li. They're just doing their job. Just routine stuff for police investigations. Nothing personal."

"To watch my apartment and follow me? Feels real personal to me." She was a renowned international musician welcomed all over the world, not a police suspect. Or at least she thought of herself that way.

To know that the police thought her a suspect and others a target was crazy. She swallowed. And true.

CHAPTER TEN

Nick slowed the truck. "At the intersection."

"You just passed us. We'll tail the Taurus and keep a safe distance."

Emily tried to sort everything out. She was considered a musical genius, but these shocking events and negotiating the labyrinth of suspicions had her paralyzed. The police believed that she was capable of killing two men whom she cared about. What could they possibly imagine was her motive? She watched crime shows. The motive was essential to solving a crime.

Stella burrowed herself into Emily's lap. The dog was an empath, giving Emily comfort right when she needed it.

"How are you two holding up? It's a lot to take in."

Nick reached out and rubbed along her tight fist with his calloused fingertips, forcing her to remember how tender and gentle he could be despite his size. Rather like the man, opposing forces of stubborn and caring. She had resolved to abandon the conundrum of Nick Jenkins.

"You're safe, Emily. I won't let anyone hurt you or Stella."

She wished she could feel comforted by Nick's promise. He meant everything he said, but his body language registered off the Richter scale of tension.

"Good. We're good. Aren't we, Stella?" Emily rubbed Stella's soft ears. Stella looked up at Emily in expectation. Did Stella sense the lie? She wasn't a withering flower who would fall apart. She needed Nick to get her to the airport, then Reeves and Izzy would help her sort out this mess.

Nick and Stella both knew she needed support. And why shouldn't she need reassurance? Two friends had been murdered, she was considered a suspect, and her bodyguard who had shattered her heart into little smithereens was sitting next to her while they were being followed by unknown assailants.

"I'm still trying to wrap my head around the idea that the police could consider me a killer." Emily was impressed by how logical she was sounding—cool and self-sufficient. Not in a "is my hair turning white" voice.

"I shouldn't have told you, but I didn't want you to think the bad guys were following us."

"I don't want to be shielded from the truth. I can handle whatever this is. Promise me you'll tell me what's happening and not keep me in the dark."

"Sure." Nick turned his gaze to the center mirror.

Emily stared at the dark stubble on Nick's forceful chin, remembering how it felt against her sensitive fingers. The memory of the contrast of rough stubble next to the smoothness of his neck was embedded in her highly aware fingertips and, like the man, not easily forgotten. And damn it, she'd asked him to kiss her.

"But my first job is to keep you safe." He checked both side mirrors.

"Okay. And thanks for all of this." She spread her hands. "Whatever this is."

Emily wanted to apologize for how patronizing she had been last night, but knowing Tanner and Carter were listening stopped her. She could apologize to Nick before she got on the plane.

She shouldn't want Nick to leave San Francisco and his friends. She didn't want to depend on Nick Jenkins. But right now, she trusted Nick with her safety. Just not the safety of her heart. She had barely recovered from the last time they were together. She didn't know what would happen when Nick Jenkins walked away from her again. And he would walk. She knew just as well as she knew Pachelbel's "Canon," a beginner cellist's piece, that Nick would move on to the next challenge.

They drove in silence, Emily's brain whizzing, fueling her anxiety. She, like Reeves, was able to put a capital "W" in worries.

"We are almost there. You and Stella will soon be secure in the plane and all this will be behind you." As if she would forget her friends' murders and this frantic escape.

Emily checked the side mirror. "Is the police car still following us?"

"Yes. And it's just a conjecture who might be in the black sedan."

"I like the idea that it's the police instead of the alternative."

Nick peered in the rearview mirror, the tension suddenly palpable in the car. "Do you see that, Tanner?"

"Yep. You picked up a black Escalade with tinted windows," Tanner confirmed. "This just got interesting."

Emily gulped down the panic beginning to engulf her. "Someone else is following us?"

"Yes." Nick delivered the information as if commenting on the chance of rain. The man was unflappable. His cool attitude irritated her since she had not one iota of calm.

Emily looked again at the side mirror. She couldn't see the black mega-vehicle.

"Is the bad guy's car behind the police car?" There was a hitch in her voice from her labored breathing.

"The Escalade is in front of the Taurus." Nick kept his vigilant watch on each mirror.

"Okay. Is that a good thing?"

"What's the play here, Duty?" Tanner asked.

"Were not going to engage. I'm still heading straight to the airport. Have Carter alert Logan and Dylan about the tail."

"Already did," Carter said. "Your brothers have arrived too. So, we're covered."

"What the hell? Now they think I need a nursemaid?" Emily jumped with Nick's sudden shout.

"Man, you've got to chill about your brothers. They're kick-ass marines to call on if we get into a firefight. They hopped a ride on the Dean plane. I have to say, it's nice to have your brother marry a billionaire's daughter."

"Are all of them here?" Nick growled while still checking his mirrors.

"They still getting on your ass about your hearing loss?"

"Shut the fuck up, Carter," Tanner growled. "Captain doesn't talk about it with anyone. The twins are here. Finn stayed in Seattle to help Reeves out."

Nick had a hearing loss? He'd never shared anything about it. She did notice he sometimes tilted his head or leaned forward. He must hate having any sign of what he would perceive as weakness. The man was all about control.

Underneath his hard core, Nick could be caring and gentle. It was evident by the way he took care of Stella. He carried the dog around and talked baby talk to her when he didn't think Emily could hear. She'd believed at the time that she could come to love that man.

She needed to remain focused. The weird part of the brain was how it could bring up random thoughts to protect a person from freaking out. She had experienced that in her early days of performing.

"Who do you think is in the Escalade?" She needed to hear Nick's logic since all she could come up with was that the driver wanted to kill her like he had Yuen Li and Charles. Not exactly a calming approach.

"I don't know yet, Emily. But trust me, I'll sort this out. No one is going to get to you."

"The Escalade is picking up speed," Tanner noted.

"Yeah, I see that." Nick's voice was clipped.

"We're going to move behind the Escalade," Tanner said.

"Emily, tighten your seat belt and hold onto Stella. Brace one arm in the strap so you don't get thrown."

Emily wished she had Stella in a safety harness to secure her in the back seat. "I have Stella." She tightened her arm around the roly-poly body with her left arm, bringing Stella close to her chest before reaching for the strap.

Nick glanced over at them and then punched the accelerator, throwing Emily and Stella against the seat with what felt like g-force. Emily tried to see what was happening out of her side mirror, but the Escalade wasn't visible in the mirror.

"We're going in for a TVI on the Escalade." Tanner's voice echoed in the car.

"Copy that," Nick said.

"Nick, what is happening?"

"The guys are going to stop the Escalade from getting any closer to us so we can get to the airport. They are doing a Target Value Intervention."

Emily tightened her hold on Stella when she heard the squealing tires. She looked out the side mirror and watched as the Escalade veered off the road with the sedan following. The sedan hit the rear end of the Escalade, causing the top-heavy car to spin and then stop suddenly.

"Oh, my God. Nick, the sedan caused the Escalade to spin out of control."

Tanner's loud laugh filled the car. "Didn't see that coming. I think your theory about law enforcement is right on, Duty."

"What's the play here? Do you want us to engage?" Carter asked.

"No. Getting to the airport is more important. But damn, I do want to know who the hell these guys are."

Emily startled with the roar of the airplane engines overhead as Nick drove through a steel fenced gate. He sped through the empty lot toward a waiting jet.

"The police did the maneuver to stop the Escalade from doing the same thing to us?"

"It sure looks like it." Nick kept checking his mirror. "Tanner, I need full coverage to get Emily up the stairs to the plane."

"The twins are already in position. The rear is covered. Dylan and Logan will secure the perimeter."

Nick pulled up directly in front of the gate. Emily looked up the stairs where one of Nick's twin brothers stood in a protective vest with a rifle, his head swiveling.

Emily startled when another brother, in the same protective vest with a rifle in his hand, appeared outside her door.

She heard the squealing of tires. Tanner had pulled his SUV perpendicular to the truck, blocking the path to the stairwell.

"Emily, I want you to go with Lars. I'll bring Stella once you're on the plane."

Emily turned toward Nick, wanting to touch him, thank him for appearing when he did. She couldn't think about the what-ifs right now. That would come later.

"Okay."

"Don't worry. I won't let anything happen to Stella." Emily didn't protest. She knew panic must be radiating off her. She wasn't afraid for Stella. She was afraid for Nick, his brothers, and his team. They all were putting themselves in harm's way for her.

"A couple of minutes and you'll be drinking your coffee on your way to see Izzy and Reeves."

Lars opened her door. "Hi, Emily. You ready to head to Seattle?" His voice wasn't the same deep timbre as Nick's tessitura but it was definitely a rich bass. Emily focused on the difference in their voices rather than the imposing rifle gripped by the smiling man who resembled Nick.

Emily twisted toward Nick before she exited the car.

"I'm sorry that I involved you in all of this."

"You forgot my promise." Nick reached for her, pulling her close, and kissed her, to mark her as his. Taking possession, he melded his lips against hers, his tongue surging inside and stroking her mouth. He retreated, and his lips brushed hers gently. "You did real good, honey. Just a few more feet and you'll be safely in the plane."

With shaky knees, Emily slid out of the truck and walked toward the stairs. She could lie to herself, but it was the promise in Nick's kiss that left her wobblier than the threat of being shot.

CHAPTER ELEVEN

He was insane. What was he thinking, kissing Emily? But as he had learned over the years, you had to grab opportunities when they presented. Despite the danger, he had kissed Emily. Kissed her like he had wanted, claiming her as she'd asked him to in her sleep. He didn't regret the kiss, but Emily would be pissed that she'd responded. And why did the thought of Emily's hot anger make him grin?

Climbing out of the truck, Nick tucked Stella under his left arm like an oversized slippery football. In his right hand, he held his SIG as he took a position at the front of the truck to cover Lars as Tanner and Carter moved to the other side. Dylan and Gray had secured the outer perimeter.

His muscles tensed as he watched Emily, exposed and vulnerable despite having Sten and Lars guarding from above and below, climb the last two steps. Nick ignored the blast of adrenaline, remaining in control even though he was unable to slow his heart rate. He was trained to regulate his body's reaction to stress, but not with Emily's life in danger. She was too important, too sensitive, and too beautiful.

He released his breath as she disappeared into the plane with Lars. Nick scanned the area one last time. The lot was empty with no visible threat. Emily was safe for now.

She'd apologized for involving him as she climbed out of the truck. He should be insulted, but she'd had a lot thrown at her since she returned to the States. She might not understand, but he would always protect her.

Sten gave Nick a thumbs-up once Emily had disappeared into the plane.

Damn the twins for showing up. His team could have handled Emily's departure. Now the private time that Nick had planned to have inflight with Emily was gone. Tanner would have known to give Nick space, but not the twins. He loved his family, but right now, he'd like to love them from afar. Though having the twins protecting Emily reassured him.

Stella started to squirm in his arms. Realizing Stella had missed her morning walk, Nick rechecked the space before placing Stella on the ground. She yipped and danced before she ran a few feet away to the side of the jetway to relieve herself. Nick tracked her movements in case he needed to use the eco bag he had stuffed into his pocket before leaving the apartment.

"Feel better, Stella?" Tanner bent to pet the dog when she came rushing toward the men. The team had all taken turns walking Stella during the time they'd guarded Emily.

The dog went to each team member, joyfully greeting them by raising her two front legs and smiling with her teeth protruding from her overbite.

"Rough morning for you, huh, little girl?" Carter crooned to the dog.

Nick looked at the men smiling at Stella. "Thanks, guys, for the assistance. Couldn't have done it without you."

The only response was Tanner's grunt. None of his team expected thanks for helping a brother out.

"What the hell do you think Emily got herself into? Is this the North Koreans or the Russians coming after her again?" Tanner ran his hand through his carrottop.

"I had the same thought. But why come after her now? And why Emily?" Nick shook his head. "They were after Izzy's AI. Emily was collateral damage."

"To get to Izzy again? You better find out what the IT genius is working on."

Grayson made a good point. All Nick knew was that Izzy was consulting on a secret project for the NSA. She wouldn't apply for a full-time job until her role as the key witness against her ex was over. The amount of time a trial took was eye-opening. Especially for something this involved.

"Or to get to you? You've made a lot of enemies over the years." Dylan lifted his shaggy brows.

Nick didn't need Dylan to remind him of the covert ops he had run for Uncle Sam that had slotted him on a few terrorists' hit lists. "Why would they come after Emily because of me?"

The men all rolled their eyes.

"And why does the bear shit in the woods?" Carter grinned, running his finger along his jaw as if pondering life's deepest secrets.

Tanner shoved Carter. "What is your problem, man?"

"I don't see any link. To kill Emily's manager and driver feels really personal to her." Nick brushed his neck, trying to ease the prickles running up his spine, not liking how personal it was to Emily. But what could she, a classical musician, have possibly done to get on the radar of serious criminals?

"Don't you think that was the San Francisco police in the Taurus?" Grayson stared into the distance. His tone implied that he, as CIA, already had the answers but wanted everyone to reinforce his brilliant supposition.

"When I saw the Taurus in front of Emily's apartment, I assumed it was local police. Now, I'm not sure. I never asked Emily if the police told her to remain in town. I expect we'll find out soon enough."

Stella now planted her two front feet on the jetway stairs and was trying to raise her fat rump to climb. Her short legs, her weight distribution, and gravity were working against her. She looked at Nick and yelped.

"You need some help?"

Nick walked toward Stella and tossed some words over his shoulder. "I'll be in touch."

Then he remembered Emily's cello and bag. He went to the

truck and grabbed both before he tossed the truck keys to Logan. "Not a scratch." Logan acknowledged his gesture with a smile before taking Nick's bag out of Carter's vehicle. Luckily, he hadn't even unpacked.

Slinging the bags over his shoulder, Nick lifted Stella into his arms and climbed the stairs, intending to comfort Emily. His plan for his brothers was simply to ignore them.

Nick walked into the cabin to find the twins and Emily huddled together in the front while Izzy and Dani stood in the back of the plane. Why the hell was Dani here? She was a close friend of Reeves's but not of Emily's. The bombshell blonde in a short leather skirt and high boots held a champagne bottle in one hand. And why had Sten brought Izzy? What if there had been a shootout? What the hell was he thinking? Hadn't he learned anything from Nick or the military?

Was he the only one who didn't consider this a party plane headed to Vegas? He could feel the vein throbbing in his forehead.

Emily and the twins stopped speaking once he entered the plane. The twins' guilty expressions triggered his body to tighten defensively. Nick transitioned into older brother/ military commander posture. His stance stiffened with his shoulders pulled back and his chin thrust forward.

Emily rushed toward him and took Stella out of his arms. She rubbed Stella's double chin. "You okay, sweetheart?"

Nick shut down the image that Emily was speaking to him, comforting him with soft words and soft touches.

Avoiding Nick's eyes, Emily finally looked up after she released Stella, who immediately raced to the back of the plane to greet the women.

"I don't know what would have happened if you hadn't been in San Francisco. Thank you. I've talked with your brothers. We all agree that you don't need to accompany me to Seattle. I don't want to interrupt your time with your team."

Nick reeled as the one-two was delivered to his gut. "No fucking way. What have these assholes told you?" Emily was not to be included in the debate of whether Nick needed R&R.

Emily's eyes locked on his. "They didn't tell me anything."

Nick's fury exploded through his body. They had obviously discussed his burnout despite Emily's denial. He fisted his hands into tight balls. He was going to tear each twin apart, piece by piece.

"Man, chill." Sten held up his hands. "Emily asked if it was necessary for you to leave San Francisco. We told her that you can decide for yourself. But we can handle her security."

Nick looked between the twins, who always covered each other's backs. He stepped closer to Lars, crowding him. Lars swallowed hard but held his ground. Yeah, Lars should recognize the extent of Nick's rage.

Emily grabbed Nick's arm, turning him toward her. "It's true. I did ask them if they could guard me until I get to Reeves."

"Hey, Sten and I are innocent bystanders." Lars held up his hands, mirroring his brother's gesture.

"What a crock of shit. How many times have I heard you tell Mom and Uncle Harry you were innocent when you were guilty?"

Lars and Sten grinned at each other, unaware of the danger they were courting.

"Yeah. Mom always had a soft spot for us."

Nick thought he might pop a vein. This was why he didn't want the twins involved.

"I'm sorry if I broke some family rule that as the oldest brother, you're always in charge. But the twins didn't do anything wrong," Emily said. "If you want to be mad at anyone, then it should be me. I'm the one who suggested that you stay in San Francisco."

"Give us some privacy." Nick skewered his brothers with a look they immediately recognized, judging by the shaking of their heads in unison. He reserved that look for when there were consequences for his younger brothers' insane activities.

Nick guided Emily by her elbow toward the cabin door, away from the group. He turned Emily so she faced the cabin. He didn't want his brothers or the women to see his face distorted with anger and betrayal. What happened to the cool commander, the man who remained calm under all circumstances? Emily Hewitt happened.

"What's this about?"

He tried to keep his voice low to avoid the busybodies all pretending they weren't listening to every word, watching every gesture.

"I could ask you the same thing. I don't like the tone you're using with your brothers and me." Her silky hair tumbled around her shoulders and her chest thrust forward, making it hard for him to concentrate.

"My tone. Are you kidding?" He ran his hand along his scalp, trying not to reach for Emily. Didn't she understand the lengths he would go for her? That he walked away from the best thing in his life to protect her from himself. And despite his conflicted feelings for this one woman, he'd never shirk his "Duty." He wouldn't be leaving her side until he figured out what she was involved in.

"Yes, your tone. Why are you suddenly angry? I thanked you for getting me to the plane safely. Your job is done. You can go back with your friends."

He was upset that Emily didn't need him. The badass Special Forces captain's heart was aching. How could he explain his feeling of betrayal when he was the one who chose to walk away? She didn't need him when she was the warmth and light that he had been missing every damn day since Sausalito.

"You think I can resume my vacation knowing you're in danger?"

Emily studied his face, and a flicker of pain crossed her eyes. "Why wouldn't you?"

"I would never leave you when you might need me. You know me. You can trust me."

She trusted him with her body, her life, her pleasure. But could she trust him with her heart?

He was desperate to make her understand. "Reeves trusts me too."

"Three days together doesn't mean we know each other."

She shook her head, sending the dark curls swirling around her shoulders. In the rush to leave, she hadn't taken time to pull the soft locks into a ponytail. "I know that you're good at your job, but I'm sure your family's company can guard me as well."

He stepped closer, lowering his voice. "I think we know each other pretty damn well." He couldn't believe she refused to acknowledge the blistering chemistry between them. He never wanted a woman as he did Emily. "That kiss we just shared was hot. And you know it."

Bright spots of red bloomed on Emily's cheeks. "You want to go there? Now?" Her voice pitched higher. "In front of everyone?"

"Are you so adamant about me leaving because of the last night?"

"I'm not talking about that night with you…ever!"

The pain in his chest wouldn't let up. Didn't she understand what kind of man he was? He wouldn't touch her unless she asked. Not because he didn't want her, but because he wasn't the right man for her. She deserved someone who appreciated her music, her artistry. Someone she would share her triumphs with over the years. Not someone who might not be able to hear her concerts and revel in her brilliance. Not someone who had killed with his hands when she wrought beauty from hers. He would do his duty to her and her brother and protect her.

"Look, I made a mistake. I shouldn't have kissed you. I should never have touched you in Sausalito. I promise I'll keep my distance. You're safe with me."

"Oh, my God. You are unbelievable. You believe that I don't want you to guard me because of one kiss or one meaningless night of sex? As if I can't resist you?" She poked him in the chest with a long delicate finger. "Unbelievable."

She stepped back, and Nick immediately missed her closeness, her heat and feminine scent. She brushed her hair from her face. "You don't have to worry that I'll ever… Never going to happen."

How did this conversation take such a downward turn?

"I know you can resist me. It's you who is irresistible." Nick bit the inside of his cheek to keep himself from bringing up Ben. "I'm aware of all the men chasing you."

Emily's head snapped back with shock. Was it possible that she didn't know how she affected him, standing so close with her exotic scent overwhelming him? It was taking all his control not to kiss her again.

She slowly scanned his face. The morning sun poured through the plane's window as flecks of gold sparkled in her espresso-brown eyes.

"I'm not leaving. You're in danger. I'm staying at your side until you're safe."

"I'll decide what I need and who I need once we've landed in Seattle and I have had time to hear what information Reeves has obtained."

"Your brother will agree with me. I'm the best for you."

"I've never doubted your ability as a bodyguard. Everything else about you is in question. And FYI, the reason that I asked your brothers to guard me was that I didn't want to interrupt your time with your friends."

Lars and Sten grinned as Emily turned on her heel and swept by them, shoulders back, curls swinging with each determined step.

Sten laughed. "Reeves is going to try to kick your ass."

Lars poked Sten in the ribs. "And we thought big brother needed a vacation. We know what he needs. Or, should I say, who he needs."

"Shut up, Lars, or I will demonstrate why I'm the head of our family."

"You and Emily?" Sten stared at Nick.

Nick understood Sten's surprise. She was unlike any woman he had been involved with. "You're right. She's too good for me."

Nick's emotions were all over the place. He had just proved to himself that Emily Hewitt had the power to bring him to his knees. He'd almost begged to guard her. His life had been about order and control. He gave commands; men followed. He never argued. He never had unexpected emotional outbursts. Rarely got angry.

"Man, I didn't say that. Just didn't see you with someone as classy as Emily. You usually like women looking for a good time…" Sten shrugged his shoulders. "From everything Izzy has told me about Emily, she's a prodigy."

"Yeah, that she is." Nick had read everything he could find about Emily's career.

"I'm not sure about you, big bro. I thought you'd be a lot smoother." Lars shoved Nick in the ribs. "Who knew you could be such an idiot with women?"

Nick wouldn't rise to the bait. Nick was very experienced in seduction, but not when it came to the only woman he cared about. The only woman he shouldn't want. The woman he was committed to protect.

"Emily doesn't want Reeves to know about us, so keep your damn mouths shut."

The twins cracked up together.

"There is no way Reeves is going to miss the way you look at Emily as if she is tonight's dessert." Lars waggled his brows.

"And the sexual current flowing between you two is at lethal amps," Sten added.

Her attempt to get rid of him as her bodyguard threw him, but now that he had established the boundaries, he was in control. No more kisses. He could hide his feelings for Emily. He was spec ops who excelled in covert ops. He had already been hiding his feelings from Reeves and his brothers for four long months.

His brothers stood on each side as Nick watched Izzy embrace Emily. He was jealous of the way Izzy had Emily wrapped in her arms, the way she pushed Emily's hair away from her face. Izzy was talking quietly, so Nick, damn his hearing loss, couldn't hear what reassuring words she was offering to her friend. He was glad Emily was getting the comfort she deserved.

Dani was next to pull Emily into her arms. He couldn't hear what Dani said, but then Dani purposefully held Emily at arm's length while examining Emily's face. "Ben Bellisiano! You slut. Give me all the details."

Of course, it would be Dani to make sure Nick heard about Emily's conquests. She made it her mission to make sure the

Jenkins brothers suffered, particularly Lars, who'd had a hard-on for the woman since he met her.

The comment made the women crack up, especially Emily, whose shadowed eyes gleamed. In the middle of her laugh, she glanced at Nick. Her smile and all amusement immediately vanished.

CHAPTER TWELVE

Emily leaned back in the leather seat and took a deep breath. Having the unexpected presence of her BFF and Dani seated on each side of her with Stella in her lap helped soothe her anxiety. Despite endless travel, she was a nervous flier. The noise of the jets, the changes in pressure, the sensation of the massive plane pressing through the sky overwhelmed her highly tuned nature.

Fear of flying hadn't precipitated the butterflies swirling this morning. The arrival of the dark, dangerous, enigmatic Nick Jenkins had the butterflies fluttering as rapidly as when she first took a bow at the Sydney Opera House.

Damn him for igniting her feelings again—the feelings she had spent months locking in the deepest recesses of her heart. His bright eyes clouding with hurt when she announced that he wasn't needed as her bodyguard had shocked her frozen emotions from cold storage. The vulnerability that he hid under his anger and the hungry need in his dark eyes before he kissed her had burned holes in her resistance.

She had expected him to take over when she asserted herself. She had years of experience dealing with her older alpha brothers, who thought they always knew what was best for their "baby" sister. And she knew what was best for her—distance between herself and the complicated man.

Here she was finding herself softening to the man after she had vowed never to feel anything but icy detachment.

The hearing loss was new information and added to her confounding reactions to the perplexing man. Did he think she doubted his effectiveness because of his hearing loss? As if something like a hearing loss could stop an indomitable man like Nick Jenkins.

Emily savored the champagne that Dani procured from the galley. The bubbles and the light fragrance of the French champagne eased her tumultuous feelings. And how long would the champagne help her pretend that her perfectly organized life hadn't disintegrated into wild chaos? Lonely melodies filled with chilling figures and ominous runs played through her mind.

Dani leaned over and whispered in sotto voce, "Nick Jenkins? Really?"

"Why didn't you tell me?" Izzy couldn't hide the hurt in her voice.

"I didn't tell you because I was away in China." Emily didn't look at Izzy since her friend would know immediately what complete BS Emily was spouting. "It was one night. Nothing more."

"You swore off one-night stands after that married Hungarian violinist," Izzy persisted. "What changed your mind?"

"Look at the man. Broad shoulders, unruly dark hair, beard stubble, fills out jeans just the right way. He checks all the boxes for a fling and nothing more. Nick Jenkins has been changing women's minds for a long time."

Dani's cynical assessment was spot-on. Nick was irresistible and confident. As if he knew how attracted she still was despite his painful betrayal.

"You must have feelings for him. You wouldn't have slept with him."

Damn Nick for not leaving with his friends, exposing her to all the memories. Emily hated lying to her bestie, but Izzy would be angry if she heard how Nick had ghosted Emily and broke her heart. And Emily didn't want to rehash the experience or her feelings.

"It was a mistake. We're not a match."

"I can't see you and Nick together. He's intimidating and

brooding. But you realize that we could be real sisters if you married Nick."

What? What happened to her pragmatic, practical, IT-genius friend who'd sworn off men after her certifiable crazy ex, who was currently in jail for multiple charges? Oh yeah—Sten Jenkins. The Jenkins men had a way of making competent, independent women behave in ways they vowed they never would.

"Marriage!" Dani snorted. "I suspect that isn't what Nick is thinking when he looks at Emily."

"Dani, you have to promise not to tell Reeves." Reeves was already upset. "You know how overprotective he is. And I don't want any trouble between him and Nick since they work together. It was a hookup. Nothing more." Oh, what a tangled web we weave when first we practice to deceive! She usually agreed with Sir Walter Scott that lying was never a good thing, but these were trying times.

Izzy and Dani would freak out if Emily shared that Nick thought the reason she didn't want him guarding her was because she couldn't resist him. She'd perform nude at Carnegie Hall before she admitted that there was some truth to his statement. She still had a small trace, a tiny remnant of desire for him.

She should be focused on who wanted to kill her and not on who was guarding her. But Nick Jenkins's appearance, when her world was already spinning against gravity, made drinking champagne the perfect escape.

"Good luck with that, honey. Nick doesn't look like he thinks it's finished." Dani crossed her hands over her chest covered in a tight black turtleneck. "You know I'm team sisterhood, but Reeves isn't an idiot, and the electric vibes between Nick and you are pretty obvious."

Dealing with Nick and his confusing messages was enough without dealing with Reeves, who still treated her like a fragile flower because she was an "artist." She was supposed to be in Seattle to relax. Everything had been planned—the spa, the facials, the pedicures, and time with her best friend, away from all the pressures of performing.

"Speaking of Reeves, I texted him that you were safely on the plane, but he wanted to talk with you once we were airborne. We've been working on your safe house in Seattle." Dani took out her phone from her purse.

"We'll have to wait to have our girlfriend stay at the Four Seasons." Izzy patted Emily's hand. "It's too much of a threat risk." Threat risk? Emily stared at Izzy, then scanned the beautiful private jet with its buttery leather seats and wood panels. Sometimes after a grueling schedule with performances back to back, Emily became a bit disoriented—like "Where am I? What city am I in? What venue am I performing at tonight?"

Today was different. She didn't have her music, her anchor in the altered universe. Her closest friend spoke like a spy. Nick Jenkins stood a few feet away, staring at her with his intense gaze challenging her to remember his kiss. She'd had to sneak out of her apartment with Nick because men were following her. Possibly wanting to kill her. Two people she knew had died in the past three days.

Izzy squeezed Emily's hand. "I can't believe this is happening again. After the insanity with my ex, I never thought— I'm so sorry. You have the best team guarding you. I should know since they saved my life."

Emily hadn't had a lot of time to think about what came next or the idea of another safe house, since from the moment she had awoken, she had been running to escape San Francisco and assailants who pursued her for unknown reasons. And then there was Nick.

She lifted the glass to her lips, enjoying the fragrance of the tiny bubbles. Just a few more sips before she faced reality.

"One more sip before I talk with Reeves. I need a break before I take on another controlling male—" Emily barely finished the words before she found Nick towering over her.

"Dani, to what do we owe the pleasure of your company?" Nick cocked one brow.

"I want to help Reeves and Emily. And *tu*? I thought you were staying in San Francisco for a week."

Nick's sculpted cheeks lit up with a red tinge. "Emily, you might want to get some food. We've a big day ahead of us."

Like a resistant child, she took another sip. Any excuse to defy the too handsome, too sexy, too everything man whose order triggered the memory of him fixing her omelets and French toast in Sausalito, explaining how he'd learned to cook to help his widowed mother. A magnum of champagne wouldn't help seal away those remembrances.

"Leave the poor girl alone. She needs some girlfriend time and a break from the testosterone crap." Dani dramatically groaned as Lars approached. "Speaking of male swagger."

"Why did you leave your boy toy, Dani?" Lars's voice and eyes darkened. "Did you tire of your rock star?"

Dani supposedly was taking time away from her work as a research geneticist because of her hot romance with Alex Hardy, a famous rock star. Dani had confided to Emily that there was more to her touring with him, but she couldn't share the details.

"I'll be joining him in Vancouver once we get Emily sorted out."

Sten walked toward the women with two steaming mugs in his hand. "Anyone need coffee?"

"I'd love some." Emily put her champagne down, the years of discipline kicking in. Emily wanted to float away on a bubble—like Glinda the Good Witch—and pretend none of this was happening. But the moment to drink bubbly with her girlfriends and pretend she wasn't in serious trouble was done.

"Black okay?" Sten's wide smile softened his eyes. No wonder Izzy was enthralled with the man. He was a younger version of his brother.

"Thanks, Sten."

His voice warmed when he spoke to Izzy. "Iz, you want some too?"

"Not yet. I'm enjoying that Emily is safe and sitting next to me."

"The last hours have been rough on Izzy." Sten looked at Emily.

"Not as hard as they've been on Emily." Izzy giggled, the champagne kicking in.

"I was about to call Reeves, Nick," Dani said. "Since we didn't think you'd be involved, Reeves and I worked out a safe house for Emily and Stella."

"When did you become part of the Jenkins Security Business, Dani?" Lars sat in the seat directly across from Dani. Lars with the easy smiles and ridiculous jokes had an angry edge all directed at Dani. "I don't remember you bringing her into the business, Nick."

A flush swept up Dani's neck. And for a second, Emily thought Dani would cave from Lars's focused aggression. She slowly crossed her long legs, encased to the knee in leather boots, and smoothed her short skirt.

Lars's gaze, which had been focused on her face, now shifted to Dani's legs and her sensual move. Talk about sexual tension.

"I have no desire to ever be associated with the Jenkins name. I happen to be helping out two dear and close friends."

Nick lowered his frame into the seat next to Lars. Invading the space across from Emily, he spread his long legs in tight jeans into the area separating them. Emily looked away from the way his snug jeans hugged his muscular thighs and repressed the image of a naked Nick moving over her.

"I know you're close to Reeves. When did you and Emily become close friends?" Nick asked.

Dani was a sweetheart with a generous soul who had been badly burned by her fiancé when he left her at the altar. Dani hid her mistrust under a wall of sarcastic attitude. And Emily wouldn't allow her friend to be browbeaten by the Jenkins men.

"I've been hearing about Dani for years from Reeves," Emily interjected, not that she believed Dani needed any assistance.

Dani grinned at Emily. "But hitting the clubs together when I was in New York cemented our friendship. When Emily lets loose, OMG. Remember the House of Yes?" Dani's laugh was in the alto range. "Those two Wall Street guys? They never knew what hit them."

Nick and Lars tightened their jaws as they both gripped their armrests.

"I'll call Reeves." Izzy pushed a button on her cell. Despite the alcohol, Izzy picked up on the building tension.

"Emily, my God. Are you okay?" Her brother's shaky voice echoed in the cabin.

"I'm fine, Reeves."

Hearing the fear in her brother's voice bottomed out her stomach like a roller-coaster drop. No matter how hard she had to battle for her independence, she couldn't forget it was because her brothers cared.

"Nick and the men did a great job getting me to the plane." Memories of the harried chase sent shivers along her arms. She rubbed them to fight the sudden chill. Nick didn't miss her gesture. She would need time to recover from the shock.

"I'll check in with Nick in a minute, but I needed to hear your voice." Reeves's sigh was audible. "My God, what have you gotten yourself into this time?"

Emily stiffened and hugged Stella close.

"Your sister has done nothing wrong," Nick snapped. "She's the victim here."

"Nick, what the hell? You're on the plane? I thought Sten and Lars were bringing Emily to Seattle."

"Change of plans."

"Does that mean you're available to help?"

"I'm not going anywhere until this is sorted out. What's the update on the license plates from the two cars that Tanner sent you?"

"Thank God. I'm so glad you've decided to take charge." Reeves's gulp for air and the break in his voice shook Emily's equilibrium. Her older brother was usually unflappable. Hyper but unflappable.

Nick's eyes met Emily's, and she couldn't hide the sudden stinging behind her lids. Nick's lips softened in an understanding smile. "Reeves, what about the plates?"

"Yeah, okay. The plates on the Escalade were stolen. As for the Taurus, I didn't find anything in the database. Not yet, anyway."

Nick ran his hand along his chin. "What have you been able to get on Yuen Li?"

Emily's eyes darted to Nick.

"Squeaky clean so far. His business is legit."

"Of course it's legitimate." Emily wouldn't allow her murdered friend to be considered a suspect.

"We have to look, especially if there is a connection to you. He's been traveling between the US and China for years. And after his murder, your place was burglarized, your driver murdered, and you were followed," Reeves said.

Emily bit her lip and kept her defense of her dear friend to herself. She was a good judge of character from her years of interacting with all types of people in the music business. Yuen Li wasn't like any of the avaricious, competitive people she'd dealt with.

"You're right. I won't believe that he is involved in anything illegal. He was a wonderful man." She looked away from Nick's intense scrutiny, determined not to reveal any further vulnerability.

"I'm working on it, but it's going to take time to sort through his business records and travel history. So far, no red flags."

"What about the police report?" Nick asked.

"Well, this just got interesting. The files have been redacted by the FBI. I've hesitated to hack into the FBI server. I doubt they'd ever find me, but I hate to take any chances as Emily's brother. It could make Emily look culpable with her association with Yuen. With Izzy under scrutiny and the upcoming trial, I'm feeling a bit hamstrung."

"I'm sorry I can't help, Reeves." Izzy leaned forward to speak into the cellphone. "Working for the NSA has tied my hands on hacking. They really frown on their contractors looking into confidential government files unrelated to their work. And with the high-profile trial, I can't risk any questions about my reliability as a witness."

"Reeves, once we land, I'll make a call to my connection at the FBI." Dani uncrossed her legs and smiled into the distance.

Reeves laughed. "Are you still 'talking' with Special Agent Shaw?"

"Shaw?" Lars frowned. "How do you keep track of all of them?"

"I keep a spreadsheet." Dani smirked.

"This is insane." Izzy grabbed Emily's hand. "I'm so sorry, Emily."

"Hey, I'm just sorry I brought you into this." Emily twisted to look at Izzy.

"As if. At least you didn't have a psychotic boyfriend who threatened you and tried to kill me."

"I guess I do have that going for me."

Izzy burst into laughter, making Emily happy to distract Izzy from thinking about her sociopathic ex.

Emily didn't want Izzy beating herself up about bad choices. And looking across at Nick, Emily would never fault any woman for making a bad choice. As long as she didn't keep making the same mistake.

"I'm going to stay with you." Izzy squeezed Emily's hand. "Sten will too."

"I've never been included in a girlfriends weekend before." Sten waggled his dark brows at Emily.

"And don't forget me," Dani added. "We're going to stay at Jordan Dean's house. Her place is updated with all the highest security. I checked in with her, and she's cool."

"Where is Jordan going to stay?" Emily couldn't believe that Jordan's security team would think bringing attention to Jordan's home was safe for Jordan.

"She and Aiden bought a house right on Lake Washington. She hasn't lived at the house where we'll be staying since she and Aiden got engaged."

"What?" Nick barked. "Say that again. Who made this decision?"

"We all did."

"Reeves, explain why you're hosting a party in the safe house."

"I don't want Emily to be alone. The team will be guarding her, but she and Izzy had this week planned. And now that Dani is in town, they can all be together."

Emily watched as the vein in Nick's forehead pulsed.

"No one is staying at the safe house but Emily and Stella, with my men guarding her. This isn't some girls-gone-wild weekend."

"You're so clever, Nick." Dani rolled her eyes. "Not. Girls go wild in a safe house in a residential neighborhood in Seattle. It will be a blockbuster."

"How does it matter if Izzy and Dani are with me?" Emily tried to remind herself that her safety was Nick's priority and not just his autocratic need to control everyone.

"Can I speak to you alone, Emily?" Nick stood.

No way would she be getting close to Nick again. He'd have to try to bend her to his will with an audience.

"These are my friends; they can hear whatever you need to say."

Nick dropped into the chair. He glared at Emily, probably pissed that he couldn't succeed in intimidating her. She had experience standing up to her brothers.

"Right now, we don't know anything about who is after you. Having your friends at the safe house puts them at risk. Remember how you became collateral damage for the threat against Izzy? The reason we stayed in Sausalito?"

Emily didn't flinch and glared at Nick for bringing up Sausalito.

Nick dropped his gaze from her and shifted in the chair. "Don't you think Izzy, as an AI expert and NSA consultant, would be a perfect person to kidnap?"

By the way his voice roughened, he was plagued by memories of his own.

Emily hadn't realized her presence might endanger her friends.

"You bastard. You don't need to upset her. Sten and I can handle whatever comes at us…and protect Izzy."

Emily examined Nick's drawn features. It wasn't fair to put him in the middle. He had been vigilant in getting her to the safety of the airplane. "Nick's right. I can't put any of you in harm's way. Stella and I will separate from all of you until this is resolved."

"Not happening," Dani announced. "Izzy and I've already discussed the possible threat. We are staying with you. You're not going to be alone after all you've been through. You're the only reason I was willing to be on the same plane with the Jenkins boys." Dani stared at Lars.

"I've always felt bad that you had to go into hiding because of me. I'm staying with you too. Sten agrees. He's going to stay also." Izzy hadn't let go of Emily's hand.

"I won't be staying since I'll be at the tech center. But I'll be monitoring the house," Reeves added.

Emily couldn't stop the burn in her eyes. Touring after Nick's betrayal shut her off from her friends. Next, coming home after Yuen Li's murder had been a dark low point in her life. Suddenly, with the love and support surrounding her, she was overwhelmed.

"Thank you." She couldn't say anything else without crying, and she refused to cry with the Jenkins brothers focused on her. Especially Nick.

"Do I have any say in this since I'm in charge of Emily's security?" Nick's gaze shifted between the women before stopping on Emily.

Dani's full lips curled into a smirk. "Sure, what do you want to say?"

Nick's probing gaze on Emily never faltered. She brushed away the tears.

He sat straighter and then crossed his leg over his knee. "You will all follow my orders. Is that understood?"

"Of course, Nick." Izzy beamed at Nick.

"Sure, Nick, whatever you say." Dani's incredulous snicker made Emily laugh. Hearing Emily's and Dani's laughter, Stella joined with an excited bark.

Sten stood above Nick and slapped him on the shoulder. "Even Stella agrees to your leadership."

And now Emily wished she could stop the anxiety rolling in her stomach. She didn't want her friends at risk, but they were all determined. And the Jenkins brothers were the best in the security business, according to Reeves. If only she knew who her enemy was and why he was an enemy.

<h1 style="text-align:center">CHAPTER THIRTEEN</h1>

Over the three next days, Nick's temper shortened, and his need to touch Emily increased. He had reached the boiling point with the lack of movement on both the case and Emily. He crossed his leg and repositioned his iPad, feigning deep interest in the article on the screen. It was a ploy to be near Emily, who sat with Dani and Stella on the couch across from him, sipping their lattes and chatting. Why did he persist? Because he was a blasted fool and a damn marine who never gave up.

Three fricking days and he hadn't one minute alone with Emily. It was for the best. But it didn't stop the aching loss—to not be the recipient of the smiles, the casual touches, and laughs that she shared with everyone, including the damn twins, but never him. He'd hoped that with Izzy and Sten called in to work, he'd have more of a chance, but now she never left Dani's side.

"Oh, no! They've announced your engagement in *Us* magazine and the *Daily Mail*."

Emily groaned and leaned against the couch, her tight tank top pulled across her impressive soft curves. The only clothes that Emily had brought were revealing, clinging yoga pants and tops.

"I'm not sure if I want to look."

Emily's thick black hair was pulled high into a ponytail, which bobbed when she was animated. With her fresh, dewy skin and her youthful hairstyle, she looked nothing like the sophisticated musician who wowed the world. She looked like a woman who could fit into his world…into his bed.

Dani, dressed in the same casual attire, handed Emily her laptop. Neither woman seemed to understand how erotic their clinging style was to the male brain. Nick and Lars took turns working out in the basement gym, burning off unsatiated needs and frustration. Jordan's house was large, but the tension of sharing a house was keeping him on edge.

Nick couldn't grasp why he deserved the sweet torture of Emily being so close but not having her. He had led a principled life, fighting for family and country, and didn't feel like karma should be this unfair.

"It's a new picture of you and Ben." Dani sniggered.

On their arrival in Seattle, the internet was flooded with pictures of Emily and Bellisiano as a couple. Their romance went viral. Tourists had taken pictures of Emily and Ben outside the Fu Bar—to reinforce to Nick how FUBARed he was.

The two pictures that appeared over and over on different sites showed Bellisiano's hand on Emily's waist as he led her to the town car, and Emily looking up at Bellisiano with a warm smile as she stepped into the vehicle.

Yesterday, new pictures emerged, showing Emily and Bellisiano inside the Fu Bar. The latest pictures were plastered on every site. A series of shots depicted Emily and Bellisiano laughing together, leaning on each other at the bar, clinking their glasses.

Nick didn't like the timing of the release of the photos or the ad nauseam conversations about the famous tenor. Nor did he like the constant jealousy that gnawed giant holes in his gut.

That suddenly Emily's face was posted on every magazine cover in the grocery store and on the internet as she was whisked to a safe house triggered every red flag—as if the men pursuing Emily conspired with the media to help in their search to find her.

Reeves's and his team's deep dive into the magazine websites found no links to prove that the pictures weren't taken by tourists in awe of Bellisiano. Nick had his team on high alert, with one man posted outside the safe house and one observing from his position in a parked car.

Despite the latest in tech security with motion detectors, body heat detectors, facial recognition door locks, and LED cameras, Nick would never leave anyone's safety solely dependent on tech. When it came to Emily, he and Reeves had resorted to overkill. Like the modern updates to the craftsman-style house, the tech innovations were done tastefully and unobtrusively. The beautifully restored house looked no different than any of the others on the steep hill that overlooked Lake Washington.

"Oh, that's a picture from several years ago. Ben and I were both performing in Rome. We met for drinks."

Nick's body tightened into fight-and-conquer mode. He was now conditioned to respond with primal jealousy every time the famous tenor was mentioned. Disgusted by his body's reaction, Nick stretched his legs. He never wanted to hear the name Ben Bellisiano again. Or ever see another damn picture of Bellisiano touching Emily.

"They're getting desperate for news if they're posting pictures from three years ago. This caption on the Slipped Disc blog says you broke Ben's heart and he's been looking for solace with other women." Dani reached over and enlarged the picture on the computer. "He's got that whole 'let's have monkey sex' look going, doesn't he?"

Nick ground his teeth together to stop from saying every curse word in his extensive vocabulary. "Let me remind you that the media attention could be a ruse to try to track Emily."

Nick was Danny Downer in the safe house. He was the one who had taken all of Emily's electronics and reinforced the rules. It was standard protection practice, but he still hated being the bad guy. Thank God she was finished touring and headed to the recording studio in a few weeks. He could imagine Emily's reaction if he had to cancel her tour.

As the oldest brother and a US Marine commander, he was used to playing the bad cop role, but sometimes he'd like to blow it all off. He'd like Emily to see him as the guy who wasn't always the enforcer, but as the fun guy—the way she'd seen him in Sausalito.

They'd been in touch with the San Francisco police, who had no leads on who killed Charles or Yuen Li. Nick had asked Logan to check in and see what he could do.

"You don't really suspect Ben? I could call him from a burner phone to see if he or his publicist knows anything about who leaked the photos. I don't want him to believe that I had any part in it." Emily looked at Nick.

For the first time since he joined them, he had her attention. And of course, she was discussing Bellisiano. His grip on his device tightened.

Nick chose not to share that he had Reeves do a deep dig on Bellisiano. Except for being a hound dog, the tech team found no connection to the leak of the pictures to Bellisiano. He'd gotten out of the car with Emily and taken a taxi home—probably what had kept him alive.

"We can't risk the possibility that someone has hacked Ben's phone and will be able to track the call. The news outlets and the criminals are most likely surveilling him to find you. Ben knows that you're too nice and too classy to use him for self-promotion. On the other hand, I wouldn't put it past him to milk this situation," Dani said.

It had surprised Nick how he could rely on Dani to reinforce the need for diligence in Emily's safety. She had convinced Emily to continue to perform her self-defense moves. The women practiced every day in the bedroom, not allowing any Jenkins men to participate. The women's rejection of the Jenkins brothers was a bonding moment for the brothers, helping Nick let go of some of his resentment about the crap intervention.

Dani also talked Emily down when Nick wouldn't allow Emily to walk Stella to the dog park. And now she'd tactfully convinced Emily not to call Ben. Nick had changed his opinion of Dani. She wasn't just a blond ballbuster. She was warm, quirky, and intelligent. And he owed her big time since Nick couldn't possibly be rational about Bellisiano.

"I'm the one benefiting. My sales are at a record high since the fake romance broke. Once I get home, I'll call Ben to get together and have a good laugh."

"Nick, what are you reading that caused that look of acid reflux?" Dani's knowing smirk indicated how she saw straight through his pretense of not being affected by either Emily or her "media romance."

"Tell me again what your FBI contact told you." Nick shut his device and glared at Dani.

"The FBI was alerted to Yuen Li's murder because he was on Homeland's watch list. The FBI didn't find anything politically suspicious about his murder. Shaw doesn't know if Homeland has anything else on Yuen. Shaw believes Yuen was flagged because of the frequency of his trips to China."

"I can't believe they haven't found a link between the driver's and Yuen Li's murders." The wait with no leads was the second reason Nick needed to punch a wall or go on a bender. Reason number one sat across from him.

"The detective in San Fran told me this morning that the FBI is about to close the case as a random murder, leaving it in the local PD's hands. Though they will probably let it go cold."

Since Nick couldn't sleep with Emily near, he was up early re-working every angle, but there was still nothing to move on. Reeves was also working nonstop searching for a link between Emily, Yuen, the SUV, and the dead driver. How long could he keep Emily in a safe house with no actionable intel? But he couldn't let Emily return to New York without protection.

"They're probably closing the case because Yuen Li did nothing wrong," Emily said.

Emily hadn't once changed her opinion that Yuen was an innocent victim. And he hoped for Emily's sake that she was right. His work in hellholes made him jaded and a pessimist. A wave of melancholy rolled over him with the reminder of the wide chasm between Emily and him. He had seen the worst in humankind; Emily had seen only the best.

"Dani, can you call Shaw again? Reeves hacked into the FBI

last night and found nothing, so if Shaw has any new insight or information, it isn't on their server. Reeves still hasn't found what alphabet agency was in the Taurus. And no leads on a rental for the SUV."

Emily gasped. "I thought Reeves wasn't going to do any hacking."

"That was the plan forty-eight hours ago, but last night he and I decided that with nothing to go on, he needed to dig deeper. Traditional channels weren't working."

"You forced my brother to risk going to prison?" Emily scowled at Nick. And how bad was it that he was happy to have Emily's attention focused on him and that he found her wrinkled forehead and her protruding lower lip endearing?

"Of course not. Reeves makes his own decisions. And his feelings would be hurt that you don't have faith in his abilities."

Nick was distracted by the way Emily's chest rose and how she chewed on her lower lip.

"I didn't think you'd object to our attempt to release you from the safe house, allowing you to get back to your life and your fiancé."

Dani stretched and dramatically winked at Nick. "I'll let you two hash it out. I'm going to call Shaw and see if the FBI has signed off on Yuen's murder."

"If the FBI closed the case on Yuen Li's death, how long will we keep searching for the men who followed us?" Emily asked. "What if we never find them?"

"I'm not sure when you'll be able to return to New York. Hopefully, it won't be too long." The idea of not seeing Emily every day was suddenly disturbing to a man who valued independence. "I'm sorry that you didn't get to have your break with Izzy and do the fun stuff you had planned."

"Thank you for agreeing to everyone staying. I know it wasn't easy for you."

Nick liked to believe this was a sign that the deep freeze between them was thawing, but this was Emily's standard MO. She acknowledged his efforts. He didn't want her polite. He wanted her laughing and teasing, needing him. He wanted the passionate woman who made her way into his bed and heart.

"I don't think I had a choice."

He liked the way her smile diminished the tension in her face.

"Dani can be pretty convincing."

"I like her, despite the way she's torturing Lars. My brother is losing it. I've never seen him act so irrationally. I wish Dani would let him down gently."

"Dani's not trying to hurt Lars. After what's happened, she just doesn't trust Lars or men like him." She twirled her ponytail between her fingers. "He doesn't exactly have a good track record with commitment."

"He'd never hurt a woman intentionally."

"Maybe not intentionally, but I'm sure you and your brothers have broken a lot of hearts…"

Nick's heart thudded against his chest. What had Dani been telling Emily about him and his brothers?

"My brothers would never be dishonest, and neither would I. I've always been straight up with women that my career was not conducive to anything long term."

"Really? So noble."

He wasn't noble. He was a realist. But watching Sten and Izzy happy together made him fantasize. Izzy was brilliant and financially successful, and she loved Sten despite his violent past.

Hard logic won out. He and Emily were nothing like Sten and Izzy, who had a new life with no barriers to their future. Sten didn't have a hearing loss that prevented him from sharing Izzy's passion. Sten was still in the military building a new career in military intelligence, whereas Nick now ran a family-owned security firm, and Emily was a global rising star nearing the pinnacle of her career. Thanks partially to her romantic association with Bellisiano, she was becoming famous. How would her association with an ex-marine advance her career or help her thrive?

"And there is only one woman I wanted to break all my rules for…"

"Really. Tell me more about this one woman." Emily raised her brows.

He had never heard her sarcastic tone before.

"Don't pretend. You know it's you. Those days in Sausalito…" Nick stumbled, searching to explain what those days had meant to him when he, a man who always knew his place in the world, was at the lowest point after his discharge. He was unprepared for the shock of his failed physical over a "mild to moderate" hearing loss. At ten, he'd made his life's mission to be like his father and his uncle. But when he'd had to take an early discharge, he'd floundered until he met Emily, a sliver of light in the midst of his misery and loss. She made him want more—to dream of a different kind of life.

"The days were so special that you never spoke to me again?"

"You know why." God, she wasn't going to make him explain their obvious mismatch.

"I do?" She sat up, displacing Stella from her lap. "It's not you, it's me bullshit?"

He hadn't thought of his reasons in that context. Is that how she saw his deepest pain and his need to protect her from himself?

Stella crawled into Emily's lap, but Emily ignored the dog.

"But it's true… I'm not the right man for you." Nick leaned forward in his chair, closing the space, wanting to touch her, to pull her into his arms and forget his need to do the right thing. "You need someone from your world who understands music and the arts." He almost slipped and said, "someone who can hear your work."

"A little late for this talk…like four months too late. And if this is your attempt for a repeat of Sausalito"—Emily stood, lifting Stella close to her chest—"Nice try."

Nick bolted out of the chair to grab her arm. "Damn it, Emily, it's not like that at all. You know it isn't. I care about you. I will always care about you. Don't cheapen our time together."

She pulled away. "You did that, you big oaf. Not me."

CHAPTER FOURTEEN

Dani walked into the living room. "Interesting news." She stopped abruptly, taking in Emily's narrowed gaze, her flushed face, and her death clutch on Stella. "Well, not as interesting as your conversation."

"Is it good news?"

Nick couldn't believe Emily could respond and even smile while he was a hot mess of need and confusion about to explode into fragments.

"Shaw says that Yuen Li's case is closed and access to it requires higher clearance than his paygrade."

"What the hell does that mean?" Nick roared.

Dani moved closer to Emily and rubbed Stella's forehead. "Stella, don't let Nick frighten you. He's just a confused male with limited thinking power."

"Dani." Nick was hanging on by a mere thread.

"Nothing adds up. The official FBI line is that they've decided it was a random murder, making the file inaccessible."

Nick replayed the information in his mind. "The CIA has taken over the investigation? This means my theory that Yuen Li wasn't just a tour manager is correct."

"That would be my conclusion. They've shut the FBI out. Yuen Li has international ties that Homeland or the CIA must be interested in," Dani added.

"I'm not following." Emily looked to Dani. "Why would Homeland or the CIA not want the FBI involved?"

"Yuen could've been working for the Chinese government, bringing information into the States. CIA might have been watching him and his activities and doesn't want another agency involved. Turf wars," Dani said.

"Or he could be working for the CIA and they don't want to risk exposing their operation. That also explains why Reeves isn't having any luck with his search. The CIA is covering their tracks." Nick stared out the window, trying to connect all the dots and how they led to Emily.

"But Yuen is a violinist and a tour manager for performing artists. He developed his business to support his parents and extended family when he couldn't make a living as a violinist."

"Who travels routinely between the United States and China." Nick, again in the role of the naysayer, added, "Which gives him great access to exchange information or technology between countries."

"But Reeves can't find anything on his travels that looks suspicious," Emily argued.

"Maybe a bit too clean… Were his files wiped?" Nick's jaw tightened. What was Emily's connection with this Homeland case? If Emily was a suspect, why hadn't they interviewed her?

Emily shook her head, her ponytail bobbing, and a distracted Nick focused on how he wanted to release all that gorgeous hair and all of Emily's fire.

"None of this explains who is after me, and why now? I've traveled to Asia with Yuen for years." Emily looked directly at Nick.

"Did he ever meet with people not related to your tour or ask you to contact people in China or the US?" Dani asked.

"Never. I've already told you and the police, but I wasn't with him all the time, so I don't know about his relationships in China."

"A reasonable conclusion is that someone believes that you know something about Yuen Li's activities in China." It was the only connection that made any sense to Nick. But it didn't get them anywhere since every avenue was shut down.

"Nothing was different than my previous trips—endless rehearsal rooms and performances. I've no idea what I'm supposed to know."

"Did Yuen Li have an associate who helped in your tour? There are a lot of details to organize for traveling between cities and touring in countries, especially when you don't speak the language." Nick considered how his team went over every detail with many support staff to have a successful mission outcome, which wasn't that different than a performance outcome.

"Yes, but Yuen was really great at—" Emily's voice cracked. Nick wished he had the right to take her into his arms and hold her. "There is a lot that can go wrong with touring. It has the potential for disaster—travel delays, lost luggage, illness, food poisoning. I've been through them all. But Yuen was always on top of it." Emily wiped away the tears on her cheeks.

"He must have had quite a team. Who else worked for him?" Dani asked.

"I never met most of them. There was a person in each city who coordinated the hotels, transportation, meals."

"Did he have a security team traveling with you?" Nick now paced in the open-spaced living room while Emily, Stella, and Dani had taken their positions on the couch.

"Not like you and your brothers." Emily laughed. "I was taller than Hai. Bo and Hai accompanied Yuen and me on the entire tour. They took care of the luggage, drove the car, and intervened if the crowds got too pushy. But there isn't a great deal of need for security for a cellist."

"Maybe we're approaching it wrong, focusing on Yuen's connections to Emily. Could Yuen Li have discovered someone on his team was involved and was murdered to prevent him from reporting it?"

Nick and Reeves had been looking for a criminal connection to Yuen's activities in China.

"If Yuen believed anyone was doing something illegal, he would have reported them. I know everyone is suspicious, but I won't believe he was a bad guy," Emily said.

"I need to get Reeves to look deeper into all of Yuen's tour associates. He did a cursory check, but this might be our breakthrough." Nick stepped next to Emily. "Once I've given Reeves this new angle to pursue, we need to talk."

Emily lifted Stella off her lap and placed the dog on the floor. "There is nothing else for us to discuss. I'm going to practice. Let's go, Stella."

She walked out of the room, her spine stiff and her neck extended, with Stella happily following behind. Nick wasn't a man who quickly gave up, but he had to question what he was trying to accomplish. He wanted her but already decided he couldn't—*shouldn't*—have her. It would take all of his spec ops discipline to resist her.

CHAPTER FIFTEEN

Nick Jenkins was insufferable.

Emily lifted her cello and decided to channel her anger into Shostakovich.

Nick dared to tell her not to cheapen their time together? She poured her confounding emotions into the rapid concerto.

Stella, reflecting her owner's agitation, paced next to Emily's chair.

As if she were the one who… The man didn't know how to communicate. He simply barked orders and made decisions without regard to anyone.

Her fingers flew as her brain whirled. How could she still be attracted to a man who was incapable of expressing his emotions? God spare her from alpha men who made decisions and never processed feelings.

"Emily, I need to speak with you." Nick's loud thump on the door reverberated in the room.

Her heart whacked against her chest. The man wouldn't stop until he shredded every one of her feelings.

"Please, I want to ask you about the cello."

She positioned the instrument on its stand and repeated her well-practiced breathing drill—hold two…release two—as she walked to the door. She didn't want to hear how much he cared for her or see the need in his eyes. These last days spent in a safe house with Nick were unbearable, trying to focus on her friends with Nick nearby projecting his hunger for her, the sexual tension between them, the memories of their last safe house.

Emily walked to the door, not allowing herself to glance at the king-size bed.

Nick had one hand braced over the door in his dominant masculine position, his tight T-shirt hugging his broad chest.

"I'm sorry to interrupt your practice." Nick was a striking man—all angles and planes— but when he smiled, he was devastating. With the darkness gone and the humor raising his lips, he looked youthful. This was the man she had fallen in love with in three short days. The man who'd laughed and told her with deep affection all the ridiculous harebrained antics of his brothers, the man who spoke of his mother with awe and respect, the man who'd kissed Emily like he'd never stop.

"You said you wanted to talk to me about my cello?" She wouldn't beg for a further discussion. She knew how much her brothers avoided analyzing their feelings.

He stepped into the bedroom. And despite how large it was, his presence dwarfed the expansive room.

She stepped back, not wanting to be lulled into exposing herself by reacting to his musky scent or the way his dark beard peppered his jaw despite shaving this morning, or the way his tight t-shirt showed his defined pectorals. Nick was all male, all virility.

"Is it possible that Yuen Li planted something in your cello? Maybe a microchip? We had my team search your apartment and your electronics were examined by Reeves. I didn't consider your cello. It's the only thing we haven't analyzed."

Emily should have felt relief that Nick hadn't come in pursuit of her.

"But he never handled my cello…" She thought back on how, after she accepted this cello, Yuen had packed it for her after she performed an impromptu concerto for the Chinese representatives of the Taixing Fengling Company.

"What is it? You remembered something?"

"Yuen took my cello after I performed at the factory. He held it for me as I did all the required rituals and then carried it to our van.

The Chinese are very big on rituals and politeness. He did pack it in the traveling case. But I've used this cello in performance. And I've never detected any difference in the sound."

"Would you detect a difference if he placed a microchip the size of your fingertip? Would it make a difference? Or in the case?"

"Probably not."

"Can I examine it? I'm sure he took good care to attach it where it wouldn't be visible."

Emily followed Nick. A snoring Stella, sensing an opportunity to play, awoke and promptly jumped on Nick's leg. Unlike the dog, Emily wasn't so easily won over by Nick's sexy voice and his large soothing hand. Emily wouldn't be won over by his hand on Stella's ears, but instead by his hands on her.

He lifted her cello and ran his finger along the scroll, the fingerboard, down to the bridge, though his large finger couldn't fit into the F-hole, and then down the tailpiece. He turned to examine the back.

"Would Yuen Li be able to fit his finger into this hole?"

"He wasn't a large man, but I can barely get my finger into the F-hole."

"What about your bow? Could he have planted something in it?"

Emily handed Nick her bow and their fingers touched, sending electric sparks up her arm and into her chest. Her eyes locked with Nick's. She couldn't look away from the hunger in his eyes.

"I never meant to hurt you, Emily."

"You keep saying—"

"I planned to call you. I can't tell you how many times I picked up my cell." Nick rubbed the back of his neck. "I was in a bad place when I came down to San Francisco. I'd just been discharged from the military and was struggling with what I wanted to do next. And then I met you... The days we were together... I've never felt this before...as if I were living in a dream, playing house with a talented, funny, and beautiful woman. And then, suddenly my stint as your bodyguard was over, and you left, headed to Asia. I still wanted what we had in those days—our long talks, our long nights... How easy it was when I was with you."

She was replaying every detail of their long talks. He'd never talked about himself. Anytime she asked, he cleverly turned the conversation back to her. He never shared anything about his "bad place" or what he wanted in the future. She had assumed that he was happy to take over the family business.

"I shared so much about myself…"

"I haven't forgotten a thing. Your crazy tour stories, how you'd like to stop touring in the next few years. You'd like to settle in one place and have a normal life."

"But you never shared anything about what you wanted." Obviously, it wasn't her. Emily didn't want him to think she expected marriage, but he'd never given them a chance to figure out if they had a future.

"Gray got arrested that night…the night you left the safehouse."

"I don't understand." Emily searched his face.

"I had planned to swing by your apartment the night after you left." Emily remembered how Nick had Carter drive her to her apartment because he had to wrap up business. He grinned when she left with Carter, who was telling her a comical story about Tanner. She expected he didn't want to say anything in front of the guys while they were packing up the safe house.

"Gray ran into some douchebags who were harassing a homeless vet. Everything escalated, and I had to bail him out, which took hours, which made it too late to see you. And the next day, I had to fly to DC for a consulting gig we were doing with DOD since my bodyguard stint was finished. And then you left for Asia. And during the time away from you, I realized I was living in a fantasy. It could never work between us. Our schedules, living on different coasts, our backgrounds. If I thought we had a chance, I would have been on it, but we lead two different lives. My work is nothing I'd ever want to expose you to. You have your music and a brilliant future. I'm the wrong guy for you."

"You decided we were a mismatch, and that was the end. And I would never have seen you again." Emily hated how her eyes burned when he acknowledged he had let her go permanently. And it was only by random circumstances that he was guarding her now.

"My God. Don't you understand? It's just the way it has to be. I'm damaged goods. You deserve a better man."

Emily paced, not able to stand still, afraid she might fall back into his arms and reassure him that he wasn't damaged in any way that mattered. "I don't know how you feel since you haven't bothered to share anything except some misplaced idea that we aren't the right match. And what do you mean you're damaged goods? In what way?"

She had replayed versions of this speech in her head over the past months. "Have you considered that your stupid, preconceived ideas that you aren't right for me, a musician, demonstrate how little you respect me and my ability to make my own decisions?"

Nick stayed on the other side of the bed.

"My God, Emily. That isn't it at all. I have the highest respect for you and the career you've built. I don't want to hinder you. I'm trying to protect you."

"Protect me? How is disappearing protecting me?"

The pain of his betrayal slammed into her chest. Again.

"I thought it was better—"

"Better for whom?"

"You have to believe I did what I thought was best." Nick ran his hand through his tousled hair, exposing the dark hair under his bulging bicep, as much a thing of beauty as the perfectly orchestrated Bach's *Suite No.1*, her favorite of his cello suites.

"Do you hear yourself? You decided what was best for me. I've spent my entire life being managed. 'Poor Emily is sensitive. Emily is a prodigy. She can't handle the rigors of life. Keep her in a glasshouse like some potted orchid.'"

"I don't think of you that way…as fragile. I know how strong you are." He started to move toward her.

She raised her hand to stop him. "I don't need another man to shelter me. I want a man who wants me next to him to share our lives, share our bad times, fight battles together."

"I'm trying. But I'm trained to protect. It's who I am. I'll never stop needing to protect you." He shook his head. "Or my mother, my brothers, my uncle, or well, most of the world, really."

"That sounds pretty exhausting." She smiled at his exasperation. He had taken on family responsibility at an early age. She had the opposite experience, always fighting against her overbearing brothers.

"How is not talking to me trying?" She stared at the handsome man who had so little insight into how he had hurt her. He believed he acted in her best interest.

"Like my brothers, you'll never get over the need to manage me, protect me." As she said the words, she knew. Nick had been right. They were a mismatch.

"And despite the great sex, it won't work between us. Starting tomorrow, I'm making decisions about whether I stay in the safe house. I remained here because Izzy and Dani were here, but not any longer."

"Emily, please. Try to understand…" He ran his hand over his hair.

That was his apology. Ignoring her until he could play mighty protector again. The only role he seemed to want in her life. So be it. If that's what he wanted, she'd help wrap this up.

"We could have the cello scanned. It would be possible to detect if Yuen Li placed anything in it." Emily handed the cello to Nick. "If we find the microchip, then we all can go back to our separate lives. And I can start my life with the 'right man.'"

Emily marched out of the bedroom, away from the man who still had the power to devastate her heart.

CHAPTER SIXTEEN

"You should tell her."

Nick could feel Dani's penetrating stare as he watched Emily disappear back into the bedroom after grabbing a water bottle out of the refrigerator. Dani hadn't missed one bit of the highly charged exchange earlier, and knowing the ballsy woman, she planned to get in his face. Dani never minced words in defense of her friends.

"I'm not leaving until you listen."

"Spare me from interfering women." Nick rolled his eyes for effect as he faced Dani.

"Interfering women who can stop you from self-destructing, jackass."

Nick dropped into the chair across from Dani. He'd never admit that she was right. He had been on a dark path, and these last days with Emily had highlighted how hopeless he had become.

"Okay, I'll bite. Tell her what?"

Dani threw a flowered pillow from the couch. "Honestly, you aren't that dense, are you?"

Nick stared at Dani's unrelenting gaze. The woman didn't flinch. What was with these three women? None of them soldiers. And none of them daunted by the Jenkins' intimidating tactics.

No way in hell was he admitting to Dani any conflicted feelings about Emily. It would be a bloodbath.

"Nick, tell her about the hearing loss." Dani's voice softened.

Shock and outrage shot through his body and propelled him into full attack mode. "What the fuck? Is nothing private?"

Nick expected Dani to say he should admit that he loved Emily— never stopped thinking of her, fantasizing about their life together in the same dramatic way as a teenage girl in love with her favorite boy band. Exposing his feelings for Emily would be easy in comparison to having his "disability" dissected by the ballbuster.

"Which of my asshole brothers told you?"

"None of your brothers betrayed your big fat secret. Reeves first told me."

Of course, Reeves, who had access to everyone's files. And despite his sister's fears, Reeves wasn't above hacking into government agencies to read Nick's discharge papers. At least Reeves didn't try to give him advice or suggest a vacation. Reeves was savvy enough, unlike Nick's brothers, not to push Nick.

"You'll lose her if you don't tell her the truth. Whatever you've done, you've hurt her, but I have a feeling she'll forgive you. Jordan and Emily both see redeeming qualities in you, or I wouldn't be having this enlightened woman to Neanderthal one-on-one with you."

Nick examined Dani's face. "You didn't tell her?"

He hoped that Emily hadn't made sense of what she heard in the drive to the airport. Damn Carter and his big mouth.

Dani shook her head, her shiny hair swinging with the movement. "Nope. It's all on you."

"Thanks for respecting my privacy."

Dani couldn't miss his sarcasm.

"This is your chance to make your fuckup right. Unless you're willing to walk away?"

Nick shifted uncomfortably in the chair, which had suddenly become too small.

"I already walked away." He'd never acknowledge to his brothers that they were spot-on in their concern. When he returned after guarding Emily, his mood had taken a severe downward turn.

They all assumed his withdrawal was entirely due to his discharge ending his career.

"Yeah, I can see how that is working out. You're both miserable. Talk to her or leave her the hell alone."

"Emily deserves a life with a man who doesn't have baggage."

"You believe that bullshit, don't you?" Dani's crystalline blue eyes filled with compassion.

"Bullshit? If it's bullshit, why did the military discharge me at the height of my career? I will never hear properly again for active combat. The IED that took out my two buddies damaged my hearing. I didn't know that I had a 'mild to moderate hearing loss' until I had my physical. I should be glad I'm alive."

"Hey, I don't know a lot about survivor guilt. I'm sure it sucks. And I'm sorry that you lost your men. Nothing can change what happened. But you're here now. Are you going to mess up the rest of your life because of your ridiculous male pride? Emily is a warm, caring woman who still has feelings for you. She denies it, but I see how she looks at you."

"That's my point. I don't want her to pity me. To take care of me."

"Take care of you? You need taking care of? Since when?" Dani surveyed his body from head to toe. "Are we talking about a hearing loss? You didn't sustain a serious brain injury, did you? Because you're talking garbage right now. Or did I miss something?"

"You know damn well that I have a hearing loss...enough to get discharged from active duty. And enough to never fully appreciate Emily's musical career."

"You're giving up! A fricking marine who's trained to do the impossible isn't willing to fight. You haven't followed up with the specialist Jordan wanted you to see."

Nick was a man who faced fear head-on, but not this time. He had sustained a lot of injuries in his career, and the focus was "heal and get back out there." But there was nothing he could do to recondition his hearing. No workouts, no exercise, no treatment. No strategy to heal. "I already had an exam. And dammit, how do you know about the referral?"

Of course, Jordan told Dani. She hadn't told his brothers, or they would have been on his case.

"You remember that Jordan and I both are MDs. And that Jordan is my best friend and is worried about you. I promised her that I would 'discuss' the situation with you."

"You can tell Jordan you did your duty."

"I thought military training was all about teamwork. Leave no man behind. Yet you refuse to work with anyone who cares about you."

"I didn't know you went to med school."

"Not even subtle. I get the whole lone wolf thing."

"You're going to talk to me about the lone wolf thing?" Nick scowled. This woman thought she had him all figured out. "I didn't know your PhD was in psychology. Ever hear of the pot calling the kettle black?"

Dani's posture shifted. She moved forward on the couch like she might jump up and try to kick the shit out of him.

"Diversion is still not working. But the difference between us is that if I were in your situation, I'd be jumping through all the hoops. You care about Emily and, God save her, she cares about you."

"And Lars cares about you. So why aren't you jumping through the hoops to work it out with him?"

Nick recognized Dani's tell when she flicked her hair and recrossed her legs.

"Lars sees me as a challenge. Like every other man."

"You underestimate my brother."

"Like you underestimate Emily?"

"Touché. But you should give Lars a chance."

"You need to see the specialist."

"I don't need to see anyone else. The VA doc said that the damage is permanent, and the VA will pay for hearing aids when it gets worse."

"Are you kidding me? That's all he told you?"

Nick tried to read Dani's inscrutable look. "There are a lot of us with hearing loss that the VA has to deal with. He did his job."

"Really? You didn't question his opinion? Or ask for a second opinion?"

Dani had no idea how the military worked if she actually thought that he built his career on questioning officers' opinions.

"Are you suggesting the damage isn't permanent?" The information packet he had received at his appointment and his online reading reported that sensorineural loss was permanent and the only treatment was hearing aids.

"Everything in medicine is changing with gene therapy. And to be fair to the VA MD, he's right that everything we know about sensorineural loss from IED is that the damage is permanent. But there is hopeful new research. There are gene therapy treatments in the experimental phase. The specialist Jordan referred you to is using gene therapy to deliver switch proteins to the injured neurons to stimulate regeneration in the cochlea. Since your hearing loss is mild and you don't have any other symptoms, we both think you'd be a great candidate."

"Can you break it down for us non-doctor types? And how do you know so much about hearing loss?"

"Jordan shared what she had researched for you. There is a chance to reverse the damage. You'd be in an experiment. And there is a chance it might not work."

Nick stared at Dani. His heart rate went into the danger zone. "There is a possibility…" He couldn't voice hope. He didn't trust that there might be a different future ahead. A future with Emily.

"If you had returned Jordan's phone calls, she would have explained. Instead, you texted her a thank-you and a promise you'd follow up."

"I didn't want her to think I didn't appreciate her effort." He felt like a real class-A asshole. Jordan had researched to find him care, and he blew her off with a text. He didn't like the pattern in his behavior of how he treated Jordan, Emily, and his brothers. Shame washed through him at his inconsiderate responses. But his ingrained training was to take it like a man and handle his own problems.

"You never planned to follow up because you couldn't risk

showing any sign of weakness. Imagine Nick Jenkins needing help."

"You know, if you were a man, I'd have you by the throat right now." Nothing would feel better with the excess of emotions hurtling through him than to have a knockdown, kickass, mind-clearing fight. Not with Dani, but with one of his brothers.

"I'm not really into that type of kink." Dani flashed her devilish grin.

"Now you're seducing my brother. Getting desperate?" Lars's harsh voice reverberated in the high-ceilinged living room. Coming from a workout, he was all sweaty, and his muscles were pumped. He was shirtless with a wet towel draped over his neck.

"Sure. I'm planning to work my way through the Jenkins brothers after I finish sleeping with all the Jonas brothers." Dani flipped her hair over her shoulder and crossed her legs.

Nick cracked up, the sound foreign to his ears. Dani could've been a marine with her whoop-ass attitude.

"Why's that funny?" Lars glared at Nick, his body angled over Nick as a power play. Lars was losing it over Dani if he thought Nick or Dani were interested in each other. But jealousy did weird things to a man's brain.

"Man, you've got to chill. She's pulling your chain."

"In his dreams." Dani batted her eyelashes.

"Play nice, Dani." Nick jumped out of his chair, his mood lighter. He felt like he had woken from a deep freeze with a newly inspired feeling of hope sprouting inside. He could see Jordan's specialist and if the treatment was successful, he could pursue Emily. If she was still willing and available. Not that he'd ever except her to wait for him. "He's my brother." He needed to get Reeves on Yuen's associates, and he needed time to digest Dani's information and what it could mean to his future…his future with Emily.

"And why should that make any difference to me?"

"Because you care about me." Now it was Nick's turn to flash her a grin.

"No, I don't, jackass."

Nick gave Lars a wide berth as he headed to the office. His brother would like to work out his frustrations on Nick's face if he correctly read the furious look Lars just gave him. His need for a fight had evaporated with Dani's new information.

Nick could hear Lars's thunderous voice. "Nick has a thing for Emily in case you haven't noticed."

Nick smiled; he had more than a thing for Miss Emily Hewitt. And there was nothing he could do about it. Not right now.

CHAPTER SEVENTEEN

Emily sat propped against the headboard and listened for sounds throughout the house. She strained to hear if anyone—anyone meaning Nick—was still awake. She checked her phone. One a.m. She had waited since midnight to make sure she could sneak into the kitchen unobserved.

This was all Nick's fault. She had crashed and slept through dinner, and now she was wide awake and hungry.

If she hadn't remained in her room to avoid talking to Nick, she wouldn't have fallen asleep in the middle of the afternoon. He was stalking her, wanting to further their discussion. And, like any confident, competent woman, she hid in her bedroom.

She also hid because she was weakening toward the walking sex-on-a-stick, his pleading eyes, and the way his tessitura voice soothed her jangled nerves like the lyrical pianism of Einaudi. When he was near, she wanted to understand how he came to the conclusion that he wasn't the man for her, wanted to believe Sausalito meant as much to him as it did to her, and that he, in his misguided thinking, really cared about her.

She was exhausted from the intensity of being near Nick. His scent, his voice, his sweet way with Stella triggered a visceral reaction that she couldn't control. Her self-TED talks of why she shouldn't still want him weren't working. She was emotionally depleted. He was not a man to trust with her heart. Over and over, she reminded herself of the loneliness of the past four months.

At the end of the bed, Stella snored, oblivious to Emily's insomnia.

Emily was used to nighttime awakenings when she came off international travel. Hot yoga, melatonin, green smoothies, and plenty of water helped her make the transition to her time zone.

With Yuen Li's death, Nick's appearance, and the hair-raising exit from her apartment to a safe house, Emily hadn't made the adjustment. Instead, even after over a week being back on the West Coast, she still stumbled in a fog of fear, betrayal, and desire. She drank wine and talked into the night, first with Izzy and now with Dani.

Emily slowly pulled her legs gingerly from under the covers, careful not to disturb Stella. If Stella woke, she'd demand to accompany Emily to the kitchen, and if Emily left her in the room alone, the dog would howl. Stella's clicking nails and excitement for a trip to the kitchen would end any attempt at stealth in avoiding Nick.

Emily tiptoed by Stella to the door. She pressed her ear to the door, listening if anyone was still awake. The key was not to alert either Nick or Lars, who slept in the bedrooms across from her. The cameras in the house would record her trip to the kitchen. Reeves's team, who monitored the feed, wouldn't sound an alarm for her kitchen raid.

Emily carefully opened the door and paused in the door jamb. She checked on Stella, who slept, exhausted and unaware. The Frenchie's idea of exercise was a short walk to socialize. Nick felt guilty that he wouldn't allow Emily to walk Stella, so he compensated by having the men constantly taking Stella for walks.

Emily peered down the dark, empty hallway. Her pulse was tripping into triple time. She checked to see whether the lights reflected under Nick's door.

Feeling trapped, held like a prisoner by Nick Jenkins, she realized that she was behaving irrationally. Nick had driven her to act like a teenager trying to sneak out to party. She resented the charade. She still had control over her choices, if nothing else.

And she refused to hide any longer because Nick Jenkins had

reappeared in her life and demanded to be her bodyguard, making her safe house unsafe for her feelings. Too bad if she woke him. She hadn't wanted him to accompany her in the first place.

Emily strode toward the kitchen, not muting her footsteps, her stomach growling in anticipation. One benefit of staying in Jordan Dean's house—gourmet food was stocked in the kitchen. And Reeves had managed to have Emily's favorite coffee, French pastries, and cookies-and-cream ice cream. The exquisite Bolognese pasta would be followed by the rich French chocolate tart. She squashed the idea that she was compensating for lack of sex with food.

She rounded the corner. Suddenly she was thrown against the wall as rough hands clenched her throat. In less time than she could blink, she was immobilized, pinned against the cold surface. She opened her mouth to scream.

"What the hell are you doing sneaking around in the middle of the night?" He loosened his grip around her throat.

"Nick?" Her heart pounded against her chest.

His lips barely an inch from hers, his minty breath caressed her cheek with his fractured breathing.

In Dani's silk camisole, she was aware of every naked inch of Nick's chest pressed against her. She felt the unyielding strength of his body and the tension building in him, matching her own.

"Where did you come from?"

His calloused thumb traced the path of the wildly beating pulse in her neck. Excitement raced through her like wildfire running before the wind. "I've been crashing on the couch."

The heat expanded between them, sucking all the air out of the space. His closeness flooded her body with anticipation.

"So soft." His deep voice rumbled in the darkness. He stood close enough that she could feel the vibrations in his chest.

His head slanted toward hers. She anticipated the invasion of his mouth. Nick was a greedy lover. Anticipation built between each rapid heartbeat. She leaned into him, inhaling his male, musky scent. The scent of Nick.

"Emily, I need you."

Heat expanded, spreading out to her limbs, making her tingle all over as his hot hands skimmed along her thighs. She melted against him, molding her body against his hardness, his erection pressing against her stomach.

He fisted her hair into his hands. "God, I've missed you, missed us together."

The hungry need in his jagged voice aroused her. Desperation built on desperation. She wanted to climb his body, close the distance between them.

He devoured her mouth. His tongue invaded her moist heat. She sucked on his tongue hungry for the taste of him.

Her heart raced, and her body buzzed in excited awareness when he molded her breasts into his large hands. His splintered breathing excited her. "I've needed you. Needed this."

His hot hands explored every inch of her body, making her writhe in need. Sparks ignited on her skin as he covered her mound. His fingers traced her wetness, teasing her, probing in his exploration. Lost to the overwhelming sensation of Nick thrusting his finger in and out, she wrapped her leg around his hip—wanting to get closer.

She bit on her lip to keep quiet. She was aware of the need for silence. She didn't want to wake Dani or Lars.

But when Nick pressed two fingers into her, his knuckle rubbing her clitoris, she exploded, constellations of sparkling stars dancing before her eyes. She threw her head back with a loud thump, her body floating in velvet midnight bliss.

Suddenly Nick's heat and touch vanished, and she was shoved behind him.

"What the hell?" Lars's harsh voice shattered the silence.

Nick blocked her view of Lars. She wanted to melt into the ground in embarrassment. She peeked around Nick's naked broad shoulder.

"About time." Lars, clad in boxers with a gun at his side, was grinning.

"Go back to bed," Nick growled. The heat from Nick's body pressed against her chest but couldn't stop the chilling mortification.

God, were they on tape? Reeves would be able to watch.

Dani rounded the corner with a gun pointed. She stopped midstride. "Did I miss the party?"

Emily couldn't miss the amusement in Dani's voice as she switched on the hallway light.

"What the hell, Dani? Why do you have a gun?" Lars demanded.

"The same reason you do." Dani kept her gun level.

Lars stepped toward Dani. "Put that down…before you accidently shoot someone."

Dani smirked. "It wouldn't be an accident."

"Why do you need a SIG P two twenty-six?"

Emily straightened her camisole, patted down her wild hair, and stepped around Nick. "I missed dinner and woke up starving. Anyone else hungry?"

Lars chuckled.

Flustered, Emily missed the double entendre.

"It looks like Nick is." Dani's eyes focused on the front of Nick's boxers.

"Do you ever stop?" Lars stepped in front of Dani to block her view of Nick.

"Not when it's so much fun."

"Give them a break, Dani," Lars growled.

"Nightie, Emily. Don't do anything I wouldn't." Dani waved her two fingers at Emily before heading down the hallway.

Lars followed Dani. His voice was loud and indignant. "Is that what you wear to bed?"

Now that they were alone, the silence grew awkward. Emily couldn't avoid noticing Nick's perfect body. The man was built.

The sheen of sweat on his pecs emphasized the valleys and planes of his torso. A trail of black hair drew a line to his impressive erection. She accepted he was irresistible. Any woman who had spent a night in Nick's bed would have trouble resisting an encore. She'd eventually forgive herself for her previous flight into erotic madness. And she'd admit she was still tempted to strip the man and make him beg for mercy and prove to him that he was the right man for her.

"Emily." He reached for her. His voice was harsh with need. "Let's go to my room."

"Are you mad?" As if crazy sex would solve anything. She hated that she was unable to deny that she was tempted.

"We're good together. And you want me as much as I want you." His voice rumbled through her, as low and sultry and compelling.

"It's nothing more than lust. Trapped in this house together."

"I feel so much more for you than lust." He stepped closer, his raw male scent overwhelming her senses. "You know, Emily. I know you do." His dark eyes, usually shuttered, were open and expressive.

If Nick touched her, she would surrender. She wanted nothing more than to believe him, to believe he cared.

She had to escape the temptation to abandon all caution, a four-month learned restraint. She strode to the kitchen, ignoring her fluttering heartbeat. Switching the kitchen light on helped her move away from the dangerous darkness where sensations of Nick's touch, heat, and musky smell would be her undoing.

She opened the refrigerator to avoid the breathtaking spectacle of Nick Jenkins in all his masculine glory, all sleek muscles and power in blue boxers riding low on his narrow hips.

The cool air streamed across her face before she located the pasta. She slammed the large container on the counter before she faced Nick. She had replayed this speech repeatedly since their conversation earlier today. "Nick, nothing has changed since this afternoon. We have chemistry. You touch me, and I want you. But we're back to where we were at Sausalito. Nothing's changed. Please do me a favor; please stay away from me."

Nick stayed on the other side of the kitchen island.

"You're right, of course. And I owe you an apology."

"Spare me the apologies, Nick. We're both adults, and we got carried away. It won't happen again."

"I promised you I'd do my job as your bodyguard. Not come on to you. I shouldn't have touched you. I'm sorry, Emily." And he left for his bedroom.

Emily shivered in the bright kitchen. She stared down at the pasta. Her appetite had fled. She could be in bed with Nick right now. Was she crazy to walk away from a night of pleasure? But what would be different tomorrow? She reached for the French chocolate tart.

CHAPTER EIGHTEEN

Nick scanned the street which led to the lake and the dog park, never relaxing his surveillance, glancing intermittently at Emily, Stella, and Dani, who walked ahead.

Compromise. After last night, he wanted to demonstrate to Emily that he was capable of listening to her needs while still protecting her. It was a calculated risk to allow Emily to leave the safe house to walk Stella to the dog park. There was no web activity to suggest that anyone was searching for Emily. No new leads on Yuen Li's murder. The cello had no hidden microchips. The risk was minimal. Although he was forced to admit logically the danger was low, he'd always be risk averse when Emily was involved.

He hadn't considered how patronizing he had been. He'd never offered an explanation for his decisions. When was he ever asked to explain himself? He acted concisely and independently, trained to make judgments and not second-guess or apologize for them.

He could never admit that he had been afraid to disclose his hearing loss and appear weak. And then she would feel sorry for him because she was that kind of woman—nurturing and warm. And how crazy was it that he had hurt Emily badly because she was too nice and too caring?

As they walked down the hill, he searched the residential street lined with a mix of both old mansions and modern architecture. Nothing suspicious to warrant the nagging feeling stirring in his gut. Nothing to see except sweeping views of Lake Washington and Mount Rainier on this clear April day.

Nick had brought in Fred from the Security Company to replace Sten who had returned to DC. Fred drove behind them as backup. It was overkill with two operators as protection detail on a low-risk walk in a low-risk neighborhood. Lars was already familiar with the park since he had been regularly bringing Stella to escape Dani.

There had been nothing remotely suspicious the entire time since the move to the safe house except for the irritating internet pictures. A random fan could be at the park and post a picture of Emily on Instagram, giving away her whereabouts. Anyone with skills wouldn't wait for a random posting on Instagram to find her.

Emily laughed at something Dani said.

Nick watched Emily in her tight leggings and oversized sweatshirt that carelessly fell across her shoulder. His blood rushed hot and heavy, remembering how soft and smooth she was underneath those clothes. Last night just piled more frustration on his already overloaded libido.

He sympathized with Lars, who had been silent and sullen all morning. Neither man spoke about Emily's and Dani's racy nightwear last night. What was the point?

When Emily appeared in those scanty clothes, Nick's resolve evaporated. When she surrendered to his touch, he had no will to resist. That she still desired him had incinerated any control he possessed. If they hadn't been interrupted, they could've talked in the afterglow in his bed. Instead, she was back to treating him like a polite stranger.

He'd make sure she understood that the rift between them was all on him, not because of any lack of respect for her. He'd never forget the regret on her face after they had been discovered. She had to believe he hadn't meant to hurt her. He'd been wrapped up in his pain, but no more. All he could think of was how to stop being a self-absorbed bastard. If the treatment for his hearing loss worked, he'd then tell her the depth of his feelings and plan their future.

"You get the feeling we're being watched?" Lars asked.

"Yeah. Since we turned the corner. I don't see anything. Do you?"

"Nothing. The street is empty. Once in the park, I'll clear the hill below."

The dog park was a fenced space on a sloping hill in a partially wooded area. There were a few old-growth cedars and Douglas firs that prevented a completely unobstructed view.

Nick stepped to open the wooden gate for Emily. His hand brushed hers. She flinched and then bent to release Stella from her leash.

Stella bounded off to greet the other dogs. Nick counted eight people in the park. And he quickly assessed each one and whether they had a dog. They looked exactly like he expected them to look in the outdoors in the Pacific Northwest. No one stood out. All fit in wearing their regulation polar fleeces, high-end trainers, and sunglasses because there was partial sun. Nothing suspicious about any of them.

Dani, standing next to Emily, did the same crowd inspection as Nick. Dani had been forced to learn situational awareness because of her traumatic kidnapping. To regain a sense of power, Dani studied Krav Maga and learned to handle a firearm.

Nick hated that the warm and outrageous woman had lost her innocent world view and now acted as if she were an operator in a hostile country. He never wanted that for Emily. He wanted Emily's world to remain filled with music and concerts. And if she allowed him, he would do everything to keep it that way.

Nick continued his surveillance, following behind Emily as Lars walked the perimeter of the park. Lars would check out the blind spots behind the trees. Fred remained parked on the street near the front entrance on the top of the hill, giving him a broad view.

The gate creaked behind them. A beefy man who shouted ex-military and a lean woman with a black standard French poodle entered the park. Nick went on high alert with the couple's arrival. He now regretted that they hadn't miked the team since Lars was still out of sight and not aware of the potential threat.

The guy's thick neck, confident body movement, and his situational awareness spoke of experience. His black hoodie, out of place on the spring day, might conceal a weapon, and the thought sent a rush of adrenaline to Nick's already primed instincts.

His companion, wearing a similar black hoodie plus tight leggings and black military boots, surveyed the area. Her elegant, groomed dog didn't jive with her dangerous vibe.

Nick moved deliberately to put himself between the couple and Emily, who, unaware, followed Stella down the hill.

Dani pivoted with the creaking gate and slowed her steps to position herself behind Emily.

Stella raced on, making a full circle up the hill to greet the poodle, who outweighed Stella by at least fifty pounds. Nick didn't trust Stella's read on danger. Both Stella and her owner saw their world through cheery glasses.

Emily was laughing as she turned to track Stella's comical sudden change in direction.

Nick scanned the grounds for Lars's position. Lars was still in the woods. Fred remained in the car but would assist if needed.

The woman bent and petted Stella, who was on the ground, wiggling in excitement. True to form, Stella had no awareness of danger. Not trusting the woman's contact with Stella and the possibility of tagging or drugging the dog, Nick moved within striking distance of the woman.

Focused on watching the woman's hands, Nick didn't anticipate the rapid assault. The woman bolted upright and swung her leg, aiming her kick at his throat. Nick's fast lurch prevented her heel from delivering the lethal strike, instead striking his chin with enough force to knock him backward.

Her partner rushed Nick and threw an off-balance liver punch. The pain was swift and overwhelming. Nick sucked air as he staggered away from the blow. The guy knew what he was doing.

With Nick swaying, the guy came in for the final strike. Never going to happen with Emily in danger. Nick blocked the punch to his face and grabbed the guy's forearm and, in one quick maneuver, snapped the asshole's arm. The guy fell to his knees, holding his arm. He gasped, "I'm going to kill you."

In the seconds Nick was fending off his attacker, a giant bald man had cornered Emily and Dani. Nick watched as Dani reached for her gun in the back of her pants. She hesitated, briefly allowing the guy to get off a full-strength hit to her solar plexus. Dani's legs buckled underneath her, and she fell to the ground.

Emily's scream pierced every cell in Nick's body.

Distracted by Emily's distress, Nick didn't hear the woman's approach as she wrapped her arm around his neck to put him into a choke hold.

Nick slammed his elbow with full force into the woman's face, frantic to get to Emily. The crunch of the woman's nose shattering wasn't as dramatic as Lars's agonized shout to Dani.

His brother was on the edge of the woods battling two powerful men. Where was Fred? Nick swung his gaze to the street. Fred was trapped in the car, surrounded by two men with assault rifles pointed at him.

This was a coordinated attack. How did they find them?

Infuriated that he had underestimated the threat, Nick swirled around to finish his opponents. The man came at Nick with a knife, his injured arm dangling at his side. Nick was at a disadvantage since he wanted to disable this guy without losing sight of Emily. Dodging his adversary, he forced the guy to change his position, allowing a clear view. And what he saw forced all the air out of his lungs. With Dani unconscious, the bald guy was after Emily, who had bolted.

Nick had to get to Emily before the thug caught her.

Nick rushed his assailant, grabbed his broken arm, and twisted. The guy flinched but didn't drop the knife. Nick could almost admire the bastard's abilities if he weren't trying to kill Nick.

In one maneuver, Nick trapped the knife against the man's side and then grabbed for the man's thick neck. He gouged his eyes. With the intense pain to his brain, the guy dropped the knife. Nick then returned the favor with a liver punch to drop him.

Nick gave a glance to the woman. He had broken her nose,

judging by the amount of blood pooling on the dirt, and probably given her a concussion by the way she didn't stir. It could all be an act, but Emily was his priority.

Nick sprinted by Dani, who had lurched to her knees, swaying with the motion. Taking in the entire scene and possible threats, Nick noted that Fred was out of the car and running toward the entrance, and Lars had leveled one attacker but was still fighting the other. Nick saw no other impending threat except the one against Emily.

Nick pumped harder down the hill as her attacker closed the gap. These men were trained killers, able to take Emily in the five seconds Nick needed to reach her.

Time slowed as the thug grabbed Emily's arm to turn her toward him. Nick gave everything he had for the last sprint.

The fear on her face as she pivoted toward her assailant would be embedded in Nick's heart forever. She swung her leg to knee him in the groin. She missed and hit him in the thigh. The guy laughed as he jerked her toward him.

The guy was so dead.

"I'm going to kill you, you bastard," Nick shouted, hoping to distract her assailant and give Emily a chance to escape.

The asshole turned his head toward Nick's voice.

Using her assailant's lapse, Emily lifted her knee and delivered a perfectly orchestrated move to the guy's groin. This time she hit the goods. The guy fell in agony.

Relief rushed through Nick as he finally reached her. Before he could take her in his arms, he had to make sure this guy never plagued her again. Judging by his overbuilt body and bald head, this was the guy who'd posed as Emily's driver in San Francisco. Nick blocked the image of what would have happened if Emily had gotten into the limo alone with this animal.

Grabbing the guy by his T-shirt, Nick lifted him with one hand, fueled by pure rage, and smashed his fist into the guy's face, rendering him unconscious.

Nick dropped the guy and turned toward Emily. "He'll never hurt you again."

"Nick," she whispered, her voice shaky. Then she threw herself into his arms.

"Thank God." He squeezed her, but he couldn't stop. She was cold and trembling. Or maybe he was the one trembling.

"I've never been more scared. I thought… I thought they were going to kill you. And the way that man hit Dani…"

Nick was stunned by this brave woman whose first concern after fighting off an assailant was for Dani and him. He didn't deserve her, but he would never let her go if he had a choice. "I love you, Emily. I was the biggest coward to let you go. I'll never walk away again."

He pushed her hair from her face and lifted her chin to stare into her eyes. "You don't have to love me back, but I love you and will always love you."

Emily, eyes dilated, stood frozen. "You all could've been killed."

This wasn't the time to declare himself, but he had almost lost her. What if in those seconds he couldn't get to her?

"This isn't on you, honey. Come on, let me take you home." Except their safe house was compromised.

"That man…" Her eyes went to the man on the ground before them. "He's the driver who replaced Charles."

"Yeah, I thought so. We'll figure it out, but I need to get you away from here."

Nick hadn't wanted her to make the connection. He didn't want her to have the terror of thinking how close the man who had killed her driver had come to her.

He wrapped his arm around her shoulder to pull her away from the carnage. He didn't want Emily in the open with the possibility of more kidnappers arriving.

His team could pick up the mess. One of the dog owners would have called 911 by now.

Nick surveyed the now-empty dog park as sirens blared. Getting Emily to safety was his priority.

Fred, talking on his cell, stood over the man Nick had taken out. Nick assumed Fred was alerting Reeves to get the rest of the crew on-site. The woman had vanished. Neither she nor her dog were in the crowd running out to escape from the park.

A very pale Dani, holding her arm pressed against her stomach, staggered downhill toward them.

Lars, blood dripping from his shirt, ran to Dani. He wrapped his arm around her shoulder, supporting her. "Honey, tell me you're okay."

Nick wanted Emily gone before the police arrived. She didn't need another police interrogation forcing her to relive these events.

Emily rushed to Dani. "We need to get you to a doctor."

"I hesitated. Emily, I'm so sorry. He could have killed you. I hesitated to shoot him."

"You made the right choice not to pull your gun. You had too many innocent people to think about," Lars spoke sternly, getting close to Dani's face.

"Nick, we need to call an ambulance for her," Emily said.

Dani shook her head. "I'm fine. You need to go."

Nick took Emily's cold hand into his and laced their fingers together. "Lars will help Dani."

"For once, Nick's right." Dani, leaning into Lars's side, smirked. Nick recognized the effort she was making to stay upright by the sweat on her forehead, dilated pupils, and her trembling body.

"Can you handle the police?" Nick glanced at Lars.

"I've got it." Lars was busy smoothing the hair away from Dani's face. "You have to trust me on this. You made the right call, sweetheart."

"But I don't trust you."

Hearing Dani's retort reassured Nick. He'd made a tactical error in allowing either woman to leave the safe house. He'd made an emotional decision, and the women were paying the price. He couldn't dwell on mistakes right now. His focus was getting Emily to safety. This attack had been to kidnap Emily, or the attackers would have used guns. Fortunately, their attackers underestimated the women and his team.

Nick tugged Emily up the hill, swerving to avoid walking by the man Nick had knocked out. The police would take all of them into custody and hopefully identify them, and Nick would finally get some answers.

The black poodle raced toward Nick and Emily as they neared the gate. The owner was nowhere in sight.

At the dog's appearance, Emily gasped. "Oh, my God. I forgot about Stella. How could I forget her? Where is she?"

Nick searched the entire dog park. He too had forgotten about Stella.

An icy chill tightened around Nick's heart as he lied to reassure Emily. "She's probably hiding in the woods."

Stella was leverage. With their bungled mission to kidnap Emily, the woman could have seen the chance to take Stella. Or was it possible that one of the dog owners had seen the opportunity in the chaos to steal the pricey dog? If only he could believe that.

Nick didn't want to leave Emily to head into the woods to search for Stella. But she would never leave without looking for the dog.

"They took her, didn't they?" Emily's unshed tears and the panic in her voice showed that she grasped the reality of her dog's disappearance. Pain and anger morphed into a stewing rage. Because of his mistake in underestimating the threat, her precious dog was missing.

The sound of screeching tires broke the moment as black SUVs drove over the curb, blocking the entrance. Fully armored and weaponized, SWAT stormed the gate while others from the large van on the street knocked down the fence.

When two men approached with their HK416s leveled at them, Nick shoved Emily behind him. What the hell was going on? Who sent the calvary? Was this Seattle police? Nick searched the men for any indication.

Heck Koehler wasn't the standard issue rifle for FBI or SWAT teams, but it was the gun of choice for the fucking CIA.

CHAPTER NINETEEN

Emily sat on a metal chair in a sterile, white, eight-by-ten room in a nondescript building with horrible acoustics and a musty smell. Her CIA interrogation was straight out of a low-budget spy movie. Except it wasn't a movie. It was happening to her right now, in real time. Straight from her attack at the dog park to a more subtle attack by the CIA. In the movies, she would be alone without food, water, or access to a lawyer. She had a cup of coffee, and thankfully, Nick sat next to her, his warm thigh pressed against hers.

She wasn't sure how Nick forced them to allow him in the interrogation. From the little she knew, threatening to choke the life out of a CIA officer as Nick had done at the dog park meant you were taken away and thrown into a dank, dark cell. This mild treatment had to be the result of either Nick's military background or Richard Dean, tech billionaire and employer of Nick and Reeves, using his influence.

No matter, she was grateful for Nick's calm presence since every time she flashed on Stella alone with those monsters, Nick would squeeze her knee or her hand, anticipating her surge of emotion.

"You believe that Stella was kidnapped by the Serbian mafia working for the Chinese in exchange for information I received from Yuen Li. And that my friend, who I cared deeply about, put Stella and me in great danger by giving me government secrets.

Secrets that you can't divulge, except that they are important. And that the Chinese or the Serbians will want to exchange Stella for me, believing I have vital information. Have I missed anything?"

"That summarizes it pretty clearly." Intelligence Agent Troy Matthews's hazel eyes seemingly hadn't blinked once in the hour of interrogation. His tenor voice was sharp, matching his hawkish nose, sharp cheekbones, and bony chin.

Nick nudged her knee, likely anticipating that Emily might be considering a thumb jab to the officer's eyes—an interesting reversal in their roles. Nick had been the volatile one since his arrival at her apartment, but in this situation, he exuded confidence and complete control, while Emily thrummed with rage, ready to attack.

Stella was gone, and Emily was trapped by the CIA. Her only reassurance was knowing Reeves would be using all of his incredible skills and intelligence to find her fur baby while they were stuck here.

"What is the CIA's take on the Serbians' involvement?" Nick smoothly interjected. "It isn't like the Chinese to use other resources."

Matthews took another sip of his second cup of coffee. "You know I can't divulge anything."

"But you expect me to risk my or my dog's life without sharing anything? Have you found out anything from the men in the park? Can't you make them talk? Find out where they took Stella?"

Matthews shook his head. "I've already told you. They're professional. They won't give anything up. We're searching their burner phones to see if we can get a lead."

"If you believed that Yuen had given me such important information, why didn't you ask me instead of risking my friends' and my dog's lives? Those men could've killed—" Her voice cracked as she recalled how Nick, Dani, and Lars had been injured protecting her. And it brought back her fear for Stella's and Dani's conditions.

Emily cleared her throat and took a sip of coffee. She hated that her voice quivered when she was upset. Revealing emotion usually put her at a disadvantage when confronting her brothers.

"Because the CIA wanted to see who would come after you." The sharp edge in Nick's voice was the first sign that Nick wasn't as unaffected as he initially appeared. "And they didn't want whoever was watching you to suspect that the CIA was on to them."

Emily understood that she had been used as bait, and the CIA planned to use her more in this cat-and-mouse game. But Stella didn't deserve such treatment. She was an innocent bundle of joy.

"You know that I never received anything from Yuen Li. And he never discussed anything that wasn't related to my tour."

"The Chinese think differently, judging by the way they searched your apartment and by engaging the Serbians to pursue you."

"They searched my apartment?" Emily suddenly felt shaken and vulnerable. After everything she had been through at the park, this should be the least of her worries. The apartment wasn't even her real home.

"They searched your apartment while you were at the funeral."

While she was at Yuen's funeral, grieving her friend, her space and personal belongings were searched by two groups of spies/criminals. Was there a difference? Right now, staring at the inscrutable Matthews, who planned to use her for his own ends, she was having difficulty discerning one.

"They were very interested in your sheet music. You make extensive notes along the margins. Did Yuen have contact with your music?"

"Was it the Serbians who searched my apartment?" The idea of it being anonymous Chinese agents versus the brutal Serbians who attacked them was less disturbing.

"It was the Serbians. Some of the same crew from the park."

An icy shiver skimmed her skin despite the airless, hot room.

"How did the Serbians find me in Seattle?"

Emily felt the sudden shift of tension in Nick's body. On the ride over, he blamed himself and apologized for the attack and for Stella's kidnapping. Learning how the Serbians found them might absolve some of Nick's guilt.

"We're not sure how they were able to find you so quickly after we had just tracked your location. Who had access to your sheet music?"

Jumping between different topics, trying to keep her off-balance, was all part of the CIA's interrogation approach. Emily's brain spun in circles. She liked to read thrillers, not play the role of the main character. All she really wanted was to return to her simpler routine of practicing her cello and walking Stella. She couldn't think of her silly, smiling companion or she might break down or punch Matthews.

"There would be no reason for Yuen Li to touch my music. And I would notice if someone had written on my music. I carry it in a file in my bag with my computer. His men only took care of my cello and suitcases."

"We need your computer."

"Not happening. Her brother took care of the electronics. He would have found anything planted," Nick said in an unyielding, level tone.

"And Yuen Li didn't have access to my computer," Emily added.

"Not that you're aware of. But you weren't aware that your apartment had been searched either."

She wrung her hands together under the table, not wanting Matthews to know he was breaking her faith in her friend. She refused to believe that Yuen Li had used her.

Nick took her hand and interlaced her fingers with his.

"Why wouldn't Yuen Li have shared the information or its hiding place with his handler?" Nick stared at Matthews. "They must have had a backup means for communication."

"From your experience in the field, you know things can change unpredictably in minutes. Yuen Li's Chinese contact, his cousin, was killed in a car accident. We assume that the death alerted Yuen Li to get rid of the file since he was compromised."

"Do you know what is on the file?"

"We don't know if Yuen Li's cousin made the drop before he was killed. The Chinese are behaving like they believe the transfer occurred, so we have to assume the same."

"They killed Yuen Li's cousin?" A shiver shuddered through Emily, raising the hairs on her arms and on the back of her neck. The Chinese would stop at nothing to get the information. Where did that leave poor Stella?

"But Yuen didn't initiate an emergency protocol? Wouldn't he alert his handler if he were compromised?"

Matthews's stony stare remained unchanged, but the tension in the room palpably increased.

Nick detected something from the evasive Matthews. Nick's chin thrust forward, and his hand tightened on her knee. Emily wished she knew what Nick's plan was so she could assist him, but they'd had no time alone since the arrival of the CIA.

"How can we bargain to get Stella back if you don't have what they want?"

"We're working on it. We have to wait and hear their demands."

"Emily will not be CIA bait." Nick pushed his chair back to stand. "We're finished here."

"It would be much safer, Ms. Hewitt, if you went into CIA custody."

The veins in Nick's neck twitched, and his hand clenched at his side. "Not FBI custody? It is standard for the FBI to handle safe houses in the US."

"Miss Hewitt's safety is too important to our agency."

"I trust Nick and my brother to protect me."

"As Emily has already said, she isn't going to a CIA safe house. You have no legal right to detain her. We're leaving."

"Are you sure about this, Ms. Hewitt? Your dog was taken..." Matthews didn't finish. Emily didn't know if it was a CIA technique or if it was Nick shoving his chair back and towering over the seated officer like an enraged Greek god that cut off Matthews.

"You have some fucking nerve. Emily and her dog wouldn't be in this danger if you had done your damn job. And I don't need you to remind me of my lapse in judgment—something I won't forget for the rest of my life. We're leaving."

Emily pushed her chair back.

Matthews stood. "Fine. We'll be tracking your number for the ransom call. And just to be clear, Jenkins. The CIA is running the exchange."

Nick nodded and placed his hand on Emily's shoulder to guide her. The heat of his large hand was an anchor in her upside down world.

"Let's get the hell out of Dodge."

CHAPTER TWENTY

The CIA officer opened Emily's car door. They finally arrived at an older building with a sign advertising an insurance company. Emily took a deep breath, savoring the fresh air. She had come close to tossing her breakfast on the drive across the city. Her stomach churned with anticipation for the looming ransom call and worry for her canine soul mate.

Nick had been adamant with Matthews that Emily wouldn't be part of the exchange. If she didn't go, what did they have to bargain for Stella? She didn't think she had the courage to go willingly with the Serbians. But to save Stella…

Neither she nor Nick spoke in the car, aware that their conversation was likely being monitored by the CIA. Her only comfort was her hand on Nick's hot, muscular thigh. He had placed it there, then rested his hand over hers.

Although the SUV drove away, Emily had no doubt that they were being watched as they entered Jenkins Security. To gain access, Nick performed several steps culminating with a retinal scan. A pacing Reeves waited at the entrance. Dark circles rimmed his bloodshot eyes. His black curly hair was disheveled, and his "I can explain it to you, but I can't understand it for you" T-shirt was crumpled and partially tucked into his jeans.

She was swept into her brother's arms, his iron grip holding her tight. "My God, this is a nightmare."

Emily hugged her brother, aware of Nick watching their

reunion. She wouldn't cry. Nothing upset her brothers more than when Emily burst into tears. "Have they called?"

Reeves had taken her cell phone when she arrived in Seattle. He had reactivated it and was monitoring calls while she was with the CIA.

"No calls. I don't know how they found you. There is no breach in our system." Reeves held onto Emily, needing the comfort as much as she did.

"Don't blame yourself. If you hadn't contacted Nick to find me in San Francisco…" A shudder racked her at the thought of what could have happened if her brother hadn't persisted. "Without you, Reeves—"

"Let's get Emily upstairs," Nick said. "It's already been a grueling day. Do you have Emily's phone?"

Reeves pulled her phone out of his jeans pocket and handed it to her. "Now we just have to wait until they call and see what their demands are."

"They want me. The CIA was very clear that I'm to be exchanged."

"We'll talk about the CIA and our plan once we get the team together," Nick said.

"You'll stop them from taking me if the CIA doesn't. I don't think I could cope with being held as a hostage." Emily needed reassurance that he would intervene if the CIA failed to protect her.

"You're not going anywhere near the Serbians. Why would you think I'd ever let the Serbians touch you?"

"But Matthews said I'm to be the exchange and they were in charge."

"Matthews can go to hell."

Nick's jaw clenched as he bellowed at Emily's phone. His dark, angular brows slashed together. Nick suspected that the CIA had bugged her phone? Was that possible?

"Is the CIA listening through my phone?" Emily whispered.

"Sorry, sweetheart. I'd like to tear that man apart. They can't hear us, but they definitely will track your phone and will know when you receive any calls."

"To listen through a phone, they would have to install Stealth Genie spyware on your phone," Reeves explained. "No one has had contact with your phone since you arrived. The phone is clean."

"At least that's good news."

"Richard Dean has already given the green light to offer any amount of money to the kidnappers. And lent his jet to bring Nick's old team up from San Francisco since they were adamant to be part of the mission. They're on their way to the offices now."

"Nice work, man, getting the cash and getting the men on board."

"Nothing could stop them from coming when they heard what happened to Emily and Stella."

Emily's throat tightened, and she felt the scratchy burn behind her eyes. For the first time since Stella had been kidnapped, she felt a glimmer of hope. If anyone could get Stella back, it was Nick's team.

Reeves performed the same sequence that Nick had done to access the elevator. "The upstairs floors are fitted for top security and are as nice as Jordan's house. I had the rest of your belongings brought over from the safe house. And the guys stopped by and cleaned out your apartment."

"How is Dani?"

"Her liver and her spleen are bruised. I'd like to kick the guy's ass who hurt her."

"Nick did a pretty good job of that."

Emily flashed to a memory of the cruelty in her attacker's eyes. She didn't want to think about her terror when he grabbed her arm. At least he was securely in custody and wouldn't be at the ransom exchange.

"Your sister was amazing. She unmanned him."

"Really? Little Emily 'roshamboed' the dude? Wait until I tell Sydney and Theo."

This was more like her usual exchange with her nerdy brother than his emotional outpourings. "Is that term from one of your video games?"

"No, it's from a hilarious *South Park* episode. I can't believe you haven't seen it."

"Tell me more about Dani's condition. She was supposed to leave for Vancouver tonight," Emily said.

"They are holding her overnight for observation to be sure she doesn't have internal bleeding. She should be discharged tomorrow. She sounded good. She's just pissed that she let the guy get a punch in."

"She can't be alone, unprotected in a hospital." Dani had been injured because of Emily's demand to take Stella to the park. Though Dani had supported Emily's act of independence after her nighttime confrontation with Nick, it was Emily who had wanted to get outside.

"She's in a secure private clinic being well cared for. And Lars is with her."

"Can I talk to her? On a burner phone?" Reeves and Nick exchanged glances. "What?" she asked suspiciously.

"Let's get set up in the penthouse, then we can talk."

"It's a penthouse?" The elevator was the standard steel cage with no hint of a lavish penthouse above.

"It's what we call it since it's on top of the building, and, like all Dean's properties, it's pretty impressive."

"I could get used to staying at the Deans' safe houses," Emily teased, trying to lighten the mood.

Reeves repeated the security measures before entering the penthouse.

Emily stepped over the threshold and was hit with a wave of intense grief. Stella always rushed ahead of Emily whenever they arrived at a new place, her tail and her rear shaking in excitement for new hotel rooms, new scents, new beds, and new adventures.

Emily covered her mouth to stifle the sob. Why now? She didn't want the two men who blamed themselves for Stella's kidnapping to feel worse.

Nick pulled her into his arms and pressed her against his chest. "What is it, sweetheart?"

"Stella always runs ahead of me when we arrive—yipping, always happy. She makes travel easier. And—"

Nick ran his hand along her spine, soothing her. "Stella will be running through these rooms very soon."

Emily didn't want Nick to stop holding her. She needed comfort after the long day and for what lay ahead. She almost forgot about Reeves witnessing this intimate moment.

"Emily, why is Nick...?"

She wiped away the tears before turning to face her brother. Wasn't it bad enough that she had just been interrogated by the CIA?

Nick didn't release her but pulled her to his side. "Why don't you ask me, Reeves?"

"Because I might have to kill you, except right now, I need you to protect my sister."

"I'm holding her because I love her. You have a problem with that?"

Reeves's shocked face, his eyebrows up to his hairline with his mouth wide open, would've been entertaining if she weren't overwhelmed by Nick's heartfelt and powerful declaration.

"Emily, really?" Reeves's dark eyes locked on to Emily's matching gaze.

"I'm not going to have this conversation. Especially on a day like today." Emily refused to discuss anything with Reeves when there were so many issues between Nick and her to be settled. "You need to trace the men who kidnapped Stella, not worry about Nick and me."

Reeves ran his hand through his already ruffled hair and shifted his weight. "We will find Stella. I'm done playing nice. And then Nick and his team will annihilate them."

Emily would like to believe that Reeves didn't persist in his questioning because of her firm message, but she knew better. Her brothers never hesitated to interfere in her life. Reeves backed off in response to whatever male-to-male message Nick delivered.

"Any hits for the Serbians on face recog?" Nick asked.

"Not yet. But I'm hitting Interpol, and I've hacked into the Russian's Findface recog program. I should get something. But the Serbian mafia is mainly on the East Coast, which makes their appearance and their association with the Chinese interesting."

"I agree that it's a surprising association. I'm going to heat up some food while we wait for the team. Emily and I haven't eaten since breakfast." Nick passed through the open space toward the kitchen. "What do you want, sweetheart?"

The penthouse was spacious, with large windows providing a view of downtown Seattle. The decor was very modern and sophisticated, done in grays, blues, and blacks with cool metals. It had a very masculine feel, not like Jordan's warm house with sunny yellows and vibrant art.

With his back to Nick, Reeves silently mouthed at Emily, "Sweetheart?"

Ignoring Reeves, Emily answered, "I don't think I can eat anything."

"It's important to keep up your energy. How about soup? Dean's kitchen is stocked with anything you'd want."

"First, I want to get cleaned up." The thought of that gruesome man touching her made her want to shower and change her clothes, except she didn't have any.

"Let me give you the tour." Reeves strode deeper into the apartment with his usual high energy.

She wanted to roll her eyes at Reeves's back. Of course, this was a total ruse to get her alone to lecture her without Nick.

Reeves opened the first door to a giant bedroom with high ceilings, a sitting area, and a fireplace. "This is the master bedroom. The bathroom is over there. It's stocked with shampoo, body gel, bath salts, and anything you need. There are bathrobes and slippers. Let me know if there's anything else you want."

"Thanks. This place is spectacular. I'm sure I'll find whatever I need."

Reeves shifted his weight. He opened his mouth, and then appeared to reconsider and closed it.

"Just give me the lecture."

"Lecture?"

"Oh, my God. Really? You're dying to tell me why Nick Jenkins is a terrible match. He's a player. A manwhore. Isn't that what you've said in the past?"

"I might have exaggerated… But I know how women always think they'll be the one to tame a bad boy. I don't want you to get hurt."

"You don't think I've had to deal with men like the Jenkins brothers all my life? Aka Ben Bellisiano?"

"All I know is if Nick says he loves you, he means it. He is the most honest and loyal man I've ever met. But are you sure about him? Since his medical discharge, he's changed…"

"In what way?" Emily didn't know that Nick had been medically discharged.

"In the past few months, he's become withdrawn and impatient with everyone and everything. It had gotten so bad that his brothers flew in last week to confront him. They were worried about him. He's always been the rock for both his family and the business. Before his discharge, I'd say he'd be a great guy for you. Now, I'm not sure."

She had been dreading Reeves's talk since she assumed it would be her brothers' standard warning on men's needs for the physical versus women's need for the emotional. She had heard variations of the talk from each brother in the hopes she'd never allow any man to use her. As if. For the first time in her life, she was glad to listen to Reeves.

"He was discharged because of his hearing loss?"

Reeves's head snapped back. "Nick told you? He doesn't discuss it with anyone. I only found out because I hacked his medical records. He planned to be a career marine—naval academy, decorated hero, spec ops all the way. He was straight on the path to becoming a general."

"Must have been difficult to have his career stripped away so abruptly." Nick had told her in Sausalito that he'd left the marines, but she assumed it was because he wanted to run the family business. Not because he was forced out.

Always in control, confident Nick Jenkins's world had crashed. Emily couldn't imagine what it would be like to suddenly not be able to play the cello. She knew of cellists who developed arm and neck problems from the repeated motion who'd had to end their careers.

Nick had trained his entire life. To lose his career over a medical problem would be devastating to a man who prided himself on his physical prowess. As a macho marine, seeing himself as less or weak would be a big blow and make him feel unworthy.

His comment that she needed a man from her world flashed through her mind. The damn man was trying to protect her because he saw himself as less than what she needed—less of that man because of his hearing loss.

Emily had hit a fork in the road. She could protect herself. And if she rejected him again, she could ensure he'd never have the ability to hurt her again. And Nick would go on believing his hearing loss made him less.

Nick needed a woman who would protect him from his overdeveloped sense of duty. He needed her love to accept that he might not always have to be the protector, the responsible one, the one in charge. That she was the woman who'd give him lessons in how to trust her with his heart.

"I know you'll get mad, but if he hurts you, I'm going to have to kick his ass. And I'll never stand a chance against a highly trained military officer, physically or tactically."

Emily stood on tiptoe and kissed Reeves on the cheek. "I appreciate the sentiment. But I can handle Nick Jenkins."

CHAPTER TWENTY-ONE

Nick heated up tomato soup and made grilled cheese sandwiches—a classic comfort meal. Meanwhile, Emily was cleaning up. The poor woman had been chased, accosted, and then taken into CIA custody and was now in limbo, waiting to hear the fate of her beloved dog. He would like to comfort her the way he knew best, but now wasn't the time.

He took a bite of the crusty, buttered bread with the sharp cheddar oozing out the sides. Grilled cheese with tomato soup was what his mother always made whenever one of her sons had a bad day, and the only approach he could think of besides the one his male brain conjured. His mother wouldn't believe that a gentle, classy woman like Emily was involved with her son.

He had almost devoured three sandwiches during the time Emily had disappeared into the bedroom. Not that he blamed her for needing time alone. Hell, he wouldn't blame her if she never came out of the bedroom.

Nick's phone beeped with a text message. The guys were on their way up. Damn lousy timing. He wanted time alone with Emily after declaring he loved her without warning. Not exactly his smoothest move, but when it came to love, he wasn't slick. Aware of how close he had been to losing her, something wild and free broke loose, and he couldn't contain his feelings.

Nick heard the men's loud voices in the hallway. He strode to the door and opened it.

Logan was the first through. "Mighty fine digs, Duty."

Gray, Dylan, Carter, and Tanner followed. Their size and their colossal attitudes filled the empty space.

"I could get used to flying in Dean's Gulfstream Supersonic X-54." Logan's head swiveled, taking in the modern furnishings with everything matching and meticulously arranged. No wide screen with comfy recliners for the Deans. Except above the couch was a gray and blue painting of Puget Sound that rotated to reveal the largest TV Nick had seen. Nick had discovered it when Sophie Dean was in hiding in the penthouse.

"Whoa, get a load of this safe house." Gray strode toward the window overlooking the expansive view.

"What smells so good?" Always hungry, Tanner would devour Emily's lunch in two bites if he found it.

On cue, Emily came into the room. Had Emily been hiding from him until the guys arrived?

She had pulled her hair into a ponytail and wore a short, red, wraparound dress that hugged her soft curves. She was barefoot with red toenails. Nick's blood heated and pumped hard. He must have been deranged to walk away. What he would do if they were alone…

The rowdy men were never silent. Only Emily's beauty could make his team shut up.

"Hey, Emily." Tanner grinned. "Good to see you again."

Emily smiled tentatively, her lips pressed together. "I'm sorry that you had to come to Seattle." She crossed the room and slipped her hand into Nick's. "I'm never going to be able to thank you enough for coming to help."

Her unexpected touch and her declaration to his team that she belonged to him energized him. He felt as exhilarated as if he were a recruit who'd finished the Crucible, the final grueling test to become a marine.

Whatever showed on his face had his team transfixed. Their gazes darted between Emily and Nick.

Grayson broke the awkward moment. "You don't have to thank us. Stella is one of our own."

"Yeah, those miserable bastards better not have upset our little princess or there is going to be bloodshed," Carter said. "Well, there is going to be bloodshed anyway for scaring you—"

"Shut up, Carter," Tanner said. "We're here to get the pup back and put the bad guys away. You don't have anything to worry about."

Grayson pointed to her luggage. "Don't worry, we didn't fiddle with your undies when we packed them." Emily gave him a horrified glance, knowing that with all the various people going through her things, she'd be ordering new underwear.

"I'm glad you're here to help Nick. I know you won't let anything happen to him or Stella." She leaned against Nick, her curves molding against him as she placed her hand on his chest. She looked up at him with such tenderness. Could she feel the thrashing of his heart?

He brushed his lips across hers and whispered, knowing the men heard every word, "I appreciate your concern." He had never had anyone want to protect him. It was a new and exhilarating feeling. "But it isn't necessary."

Her lips curled into a secret smile.

The men all watched with rapt interest. When this damn business was over, he was taking Emily to a deserted island.

"Don't you worry, we'll make sure the captain stays safe," Tanner deadpanned.

The men guffawed.

Caught off-balance by Emily's open affection, Nick pulled himself together.

"We need to get to work. I have a plan, but it means dodging the CIA. Not sure if there will be any fallout. I want to see if you're in. Especially you, Dylan, since none of us know who your new employer is."

Dylan was always slow to show his hand. "Let's hear the plan."

"Take a seat." Nick pointed to the massive granite table as he guided Emily next to him, needing to keep the contact now that she had touched him.

He whispered to Emily, "Didn't you find any shoes?"

"Yes, but they're too small. This dress is the only thing that fits because it's made of stretchy material."

"I like the material and how it stretches on you." God, he needed to get control or he'd embarrass himself in front of the team. And they would never let him forget it.

Though pretending to ignore his moment with Emily, the trained operators didn't miss a damn thing. They pulled out the modern silver chairs and contorted their massive bodies into them as best they could.

Nick pulled out a chair for Emily in front of the place setting he had set next to his. He had envisioned them sharing lunch alone, away from all obligations. "I've got your food ready." He couldn't stop himself from running his hand along her smooth, exposed arm. From his position behind her, he was tempted to lift her ponytail and kiss her graceful neck.

Emily smiled up at him and grabbed his hand. "I can get my food. You need to talk with the men."

"It's all ready." Nick's rumbly voice betrayed how shaken he was. He retreated to the kitchen to grab the soup and sandwich that he had prepared and served it to Emily.

Nick ignored Tanner's smirk.

"Thank you." She flashed her warm smile.

"Where's Reeves?" Logan asked as Nick went to his position at the head of the table.

"He's looking into a face recog hit that he got on one of the Serbians." Nick hoped they'd have more intel on the Serbians before the ransom call, giving him a better handle on how to proceed with the negotiations.

"Reeves gave us a sit rep. But he didn't have info from your meeting with the CIA. Did they shed any light on why the Serbians are after Emily?"

Nick looked to Emily, who gracefully took a sip from her soup. Talk about Beauty and the Beast. But he had never wanted to be tamed until captivated by Emily.

Emily put down her spoon and cleared her throat. "They

believe Yuen Li, my tour manager, gave me Chinese government secrets before he died. Both the CIA and the Serbians have searched my San Francisco apartment looking for this information. Before you guys did it."

"How is this information stored?"

"The CIA doesn't know and doesn't know if their asset actually passed on the information. They're going on the assumption that, since the Chinese are pursuing Emily, Yuen Li has either told Emily or has hidden in it in Emily's belongings. They've searched all of Emily's belongings, so now they want to talk with her," Nick added.

"Why are the Serbians involved? I don't get the connection." Everyone looked to Dylan. "The Chinese do not outsource and they sure as hell wouldn't be sending Serbian mercs or Bratva if this were a highly sensitive government secret."

"Exactly. The CIA involvement is not adding up. I think the CIA has a leak. Nothing else makes sense. Matthews, the officer who interviewed Emily, was a cagey bastard. I've had time to think through the interview. The CIA is using the situation to set a trap for their leak. Yuen Li didn't contact his handler or establish an emergency protocol when his Chinese contact was killed. And Matthews denies knowing what the information is."

"That's why you were asking Matthews all those questions?" Her admiration was in her tone and the way her eyes shone on him.

He reached over and squeezed her hand. "I was suspicious because the ability to find us and orchestrate a concerted attack by the Serbians had to be from the CIA source. We were not compromised on our side."

"Matthews seemed surprised that the Serbians found us so quickly after they did," Emily added.

"Walk me through this. The CIA has a mole. But why kill the asset and his contact?" Grayson asked.

"The only conclusion I can come up with is that Yuen Li either recognized the mole or had incriminating information against him. The mole is now desperate to get the information and safeguard it."

Emily's dark eyes widened, and she looked around the room.

"Talking about the fu—, I mean the fricking CIA and their fricking way makes me feel like eating. Or killing." Tanner stood and walked toward the kitchen. "They're willing to set up Emily to be taken by the Serbians so they can follow and hope her kidnappers lead them to their mole."

"The CIA then rushes in and captures their mole and rescues Emily? But you're not going to allow Emily to be part of the ransom," Logan said.

"No way." Nick grasped Emily's hand. "Emily is not going anywhere near this."

Nick raised his eyebrows and leveled a look around the table to signal the men. He didn't want Emily to know the extent that the CIA would use her to stop whatever threat they perceived—let her stay in captivity or be killed. Depending on how desperate, they might not want their mole to know they were on to them.

"I wouldn't put it past the slimy bastards to have made your location easily available to their mole to set this scenario up," Dylan said.

Nick's sentiments exactly.

Emily gasped. "The CIA wanted the Serbians to find me so they could then find their guy? And instead, they allowed those horrible people to take Stella."

Nick tightened his grip on Emily's hand. "Doesn't matter, I've a plan to stop the CIA."

"Okay." Her tear-filled eyes hurt more than any injury Nick had sustained. God, he had so much to lose if anything happened to this woman. He'd die before he'd let anyone get near her again.

"What's the plan, Captain?" Carter, a skilled sniper, always demanded very detailed and specific information.

"We use the Serbians against whoever hired them." Nick looked around the table.

His teammates were nodding. Dylan had a small grin. "We pay them off for Stella."

"We offer the Serbs three million dollars for Stella. We give them a deal they can't say no to."

Logan whistled. "You have three million dollars?"

"Richard Dean does, and Reeves and his team are organizing the money as we speak—be ready for the call."

"And we walk…with Stella, of course." Tanner grinned as he walked out of the kitchen with a stacked plate of assorted sandwiches.

"But what will prevent the mole from coming after Emily?"

Nick glared at Carter. The guy was missing a social filter.

"CIA won't allow the Serbs to escape. Or if the CIA 'allows' them to escape for more information on the mole, the Serbs will handle their connection with the mole."

Nick hoped Emily didn't come to the same conclusion that Nick and his team did. The Serbs would kill the mole if they got a better offer or if mole protested too much about how the deal went down. When you ran with thieves, murderers and spies…

And the CIA would have their problem solved. Emily and Stella would be safe, and Nick would have a lifetime to take care of them. If only missions proceeded as perfectly as planned. If he didn't know all the variables that could go wrong.

"But I can't just sit here alone and wait while you all go risk your lives. I saw what those people can do."

As if on cue, the men stood to allow Nick to handle Emily.

Dylan stopped by Emily on his way to the kitchen.

"Emily, like the hours you've put into practicing your cello, we've done the same to handle this situation. You have to trust that we're planning for success. And we will bring Stella and Nick home safe."

Emily stood and hugged Dylan, whose eyes bulged when they met Nick's scowl. "Thank you. That is very reassuring."

"Hey, don't I get a hug? I'm the one covering Dylan's ass… I mean behind." Tanner lifted Emily off her feet and squeezed her, making her burst into a hearty laugh.

Nick glared at Tanner when he finally released Emily. "Emily and I will let you get some food and then we can start to finalize the plan."

The difficulty was, until they knew the meeting place and time of the meet, they couldn't plan. That was always the strategy. Keep your enemy at a disadvantage.

Nick walked Emily to the bedroom, trying to keep in mind his training as a gentleman and the proximity of his teammates.

Nick followed Emily into the bedroom and closed the door. When she faced him, all he wanted to do was to pull her into his arms and hold her. But he didn't. He'd almost lost her today.

"What will I say when they call me?" She paced in front of him.

"I will handle the phone call. You don't need to have any contact. I'll offer them money for Stella." Nick hoped his instincts were right on the Serbians.

"But what if they won't talk with you?" She bit on her lower lip.

"I think when I mention three million dollars, they'll listen."

He stood at the door, waiting for a signal that she'd welcome his touch. Confused by her change in affection in front of the team, he didn't want to assume he had been forgiven. Was she reaching for him from the stress?

He didn't care. They could sort it all out once they had Stella.

She rushed to him and wrapped her arms around his waist, resting her head against his chest.

He enfolded her in his arms, surprised by how tightly she held him.

"I was never more afraid than I was watching the man attack you with the knife. I couldn't fathom living without you in the world. No matter how much you've hurt me, I never want you to be injured."

"God, you're killing me. I don't deserve your forgiveness. You must believe I never meant to hurt you." He lightly grazed his knuckles over her cheek, pleading as he stared into her eyes.

She looked up at him, her eyes soft and welcoming. "I believe you."

Nick's knees nearly buckled. How did he get so damn lucky? He didn't deserve her, but he'd never again make the mistake of underestimating her. "I messed up. I'll never shut you out again in some stupid belief that I'm protecting you."

She rose on her tiptoes and teased his lips with her tongue, tasting him before she thrust her gentle tongue into his mouth.

Emily gasped as his tongue rubbed against hers, and he tightened his arms, pulling her closer. It took all Nick's control not to take over. His closed heart was wide open to this loving woman.

She was soft everywhere he was hard, and he wanted all of her, now. He didn't want to waste a minute.

He lightly thrust his tongue in and out, showing her exactly how he wanted to claim her. How tender and slow he would make love to her. He might not be the best with words, but he was very good at physically expressing himself. And he wanted to demonstrate his love and devotion.

Her little whimpers and moans were driving him to the edge.

He considered the logistics of their lovemaking while his team waited. He was about to lift her into his arms and lay her on the bed when her phone rang.

Emily startled. She stepped back from Nick to reach into the pocket of her dress. "It's an overseas code. Three-eight-one is Bulgaria."

Showtime.

CHAPTER TWENTY-TWO

Emily, in a Seattle Sounders soccer T-shirt, watched the monitor in the command center. It was set up in a food truck parked near the entrance of the soccer field. Hiding the electronic observation center in a food truck was the brainchild of her brother, who was obsessed with tracking Seattle's food trucks so he could sample as many as possible.

She gulped, fighting nausea from anxiety and the spicy aromas overwhelming the space. She wasn't sure that after today she'd be able to eat Mexican food again.

On the screen in front of her, she watched Nick, two blocks away in a bright green Sounders shirt, wind his way through Seattle's 45,000-plus soccer fans headed to Century Link Field. Dodging the drunk and rowdy crowd, Nick carried her cello case filled with three million dollars over his shoulder.

Her heart was whacking against her chest in deep resounding beats. She would never forget the kidnapper's electronically altered voice demanding Emily bring the cello and the money.

She felt guilty that she was relieved, beyond grateful that she wouldn't be the one to confront the Serbians. Her love deepened with respect for Nick, whose whole life had been dedicated to protecting people. He had repeatedly put his life in danger for others as he did for her today.

A surprisingly subdued Reeves monitored all three screens and coordinated the logistics of each man's location like a stage manager, talking to each through their earpiece.

Carter, the sniper, was posted on top of a parking garage that gave him a perfect view of Occidental Square in the heart of the city, a few blocks from the Century Link Field where the match was soon to start against Seattle's premier rival, the Portland Timbers. The Serbians couldn't have picked a bigger crowd or a more chaotic setting for the meeting.

Tanner looked like an oversized leprechaun in the bright green jersey with a fan scarf wrapped around his neck. He stood with a group of male fans in similar gear in front of one of the many restaurants and bars lining the historic square. With a beer in his hand, he laughed and toasted while his eyes never stopped their vigilance. He faced the meet spot—the Fallen Firefighters Memorial in the center of the square. Bronze statues honored four firefighters who'd died in a warehouse blaze.

Logan and Grayson, clad in the Rave green fan shirts, were positioned in the crowd to cover the memorial.

Emily's assignment was to scan the crowd to identify CIA agent Matthews, but she couldn't stop herself from stealing glances at Nick's maneuvering. She flashed between the screens for the arrival of the Serbians with Stella.

Nick instructed her to look for men in Sounders baseball caps and sunglasses. Talk about needles in haystacks. She wouldn't have any trouble spotting the Serbians if they looked anything like the men at the park, but looking through the crowd made the chances slim.

The Serbians were all large and powerful with a deadly assurance. Not terribly different from Nick and his team, except Nick and his men would never terrorize women and dogs.

Her job was important. She was to warn the men if the CIA were approaching the exchange. It was a rare sunny day and every male and female fan sported Sounders hats and sunglasses.

Carter's voice broke the silence. "Serbians have arrived. They are headed toward you from Main Street."

Her heart was stuck in her throat, making it hard to swallow or breathe.

"Copy that." Nick now stood in front of the memorial facing Main Street, right below where Carter was positioned.

"I've eyes on three combatants, all armed," Grayson reported.

"Ditto," Logan echoed. "Stella looks good."

Her eyes darted to the screen, searching for Stella. One of the over muscled men had Stella tucked under his arm. Stella's bat ears were up, and her head was tilted with her usual interest in people.

Knee-weakening relief surged through her body. Emily hadn't voiced her worries that Stella might be mistreated, aware that Nick blamed himself for the kidnapping, though it was her own decision. By Stella's physical appearance and her curiosity, she looked very much like her spunky self. Like all Frenchies, Stella was sensitive to conflict and criticism, but she didn't look stressed.

All three bulky men in black T-shirts and black windbreakers moved with the crowd's flow toward Nick. No one pushed against them. The fans who weren't too drunk gave them room, sensing the possible danger.

Waiting at the memorial, Nick looked no different from any other fan except for the way his shoulders were pulled back and his chin was thrust forward. He looked relaxed, enjoying the spring day.

Emily scanned the crowd, looking for Matthews and anyone who looked out of place, but the swarm of people zigzagging across the square all looked alike.

The Serbians had arrived at the memorial. Two, with legs spread and hands at their sides, took their places in a queue behind the leader with his long black hair. Stella was tucked under the beefy man's arm.

"Where's the girl?"

Emily's pulse was off and running as her stomach did somersaults.

"I told you on the phone. Three million and the cello for the dog." Nick had adopted the same power stance.

The leader lifted his shoulders slightly as if this interaction was a friendly chat. "*Možda.*"

"What does '*možda*' mean?" Emily shouted at Reeves.

Ignoring her, Reeves spoke calmly into the mike. He had a Serbian translation app running on one of the three tablets on the long table filled with electronics. "Maybe," Reeves said. "Maybe."

Nick shrugged. "Three million dollars."

"Spare me from macho men. Just grab Stella."

Tanner snorted. Emily had forgotten that the men could hear her.

Nick scanned the crowd before he unzipped the cello case so the money was visible.

The Serbians, like Nick, never stopped looking, shifting their positions.

Emily wanted to rush out and take Stella. It took all her discipline not to go to her much-loved dog. Reeves's silence and the tension radiating off him didn't help her composure. Her brother was never quiet.

She took a slow breath and scanned the screens again, looking for the CIA. With Stella so close, she couldn't bear losing her.

The leader gave a barely perceptible nod, which prompted one of his associates to take the cello case. Nick reached for Stella, who yipped in excitement.

Tears welled up in her eyes at her pup's warm response. Like her owner, Stella rushed to the safety of Nick's arms.

Nick nodded to the Serbians with Stella tucked into his arms. He sauntered away. What was he thinking? They could attack him and grab Stella. Emily hated watching Nick's moment of vulnerability to those brutal men. She exhaled. Nick knew what he was doing, and he was confident his team had his and Stella's back.

Emily's eyes darted between each screen, looking for the CIA, not believing it was this easy. They had to be close by, observing the exchange. They weren't going to intervene and stop the Serbians? She prayed that they didn't stop Nick.

"No sight of the spooks yet." Tanner startled Emily, who was engrossed in watching Nick and the crowds.

Once Stella was secured, the plan was for Carter, Logan, and Grayson to follow the Serbians. None of the men shared what the after-plan was. It didn't take much of an imagination to assume that they planned on either taking the money and her cello back or finding where the Serbians were hiding and alerting law enforcement to retrieve the money and the cello. She thought she heard Nick mention the FBI, but then everyone clammed up, most likely not wanting Emily to worry about their safety.

Tanner remained at the bar covering Nick's return to the truck. No one appeared to apprehend Nick, who was less than thirty feet away when a loud explosion rocked the area. Chaos erupted. Nick was knocked from behind as the crowd surged. Stella went flying out of his arms.

"Thank God. The Serbians didn't set off a bomb. It was some jackass lighting an M-80." Reeves exhaled but remained focused on the screens.

Stella would be crushed if she was lying injured on the ground. Emily opened the door and jumped down the two steps to the sidewalk. She was grateful that Reeves didn't protest her departure since she wasn't about to listen when Stella's life was in jeopardy.

Emily pushed her way against the crowd to get to Stella. Her hands and legs were shaking. A drunk youth staggered into her, and she fell backward as an iron grip from behind grabbed her arm.

"Ms. Hewitt, Intelligence Officer Bradley Sabo. You shouldn't be out here. It's still dangerous with the Serbians in the area."

The skinny man with stooped shoulders in the requisite Sounders hat and sunglasses squeezed her arm to the point of pain.

"You have no right to detain me. I need to find my dog." Emily pulled away. Nick was only feet away. But where was Stella? Something about this officer was familiar. Had she seen him at the CIA's interrogation?

Emily refused to be taken by the CIA. She stood on tiptoe to see over the crowd for Nick or Stella. "I have done nothing wrong."

"You're interfering in a federal investigation. You need to come with me now." The desperation in his voice raised all the fine hairs on her neck, and she realized he was the CIA mole.

"Release my arm now. Or I will scream."

He couldn't drag her through the crowd without being noticed. Reeves was watching the crowd. He would alert Tanner.

"And what do you think will happen? I'll flash my badge, and no one will help."

The sight of a young couple snapping pictures with their cell phones crystallized a memory.

She whipped around to look at him. "You were the tourist taking pictures of Ben and me outside the bar." Her heart was now doing a fast crescendo, like the part of the music rushing to the end. He was evil, responsible for the death of Yuen Li and Charles. And now he was desperate.

"Very clever, Emily."

Tremors of fear wracked her body. She couldn't stop shaking. She couldn't move air into her lungs.

"I've got a gun, and I'll use it." He pressed it to her side through his windbreaker. "You're coming with me."

"You'll never get away with this. Let me go."

She yanked on his grip with no result. She could twist and try to knee him or jab his eyes, but the cold metal pressing against her side rattled her thinking. Any one of those moves might force him to act before she could escape.

"I'd hate to have to shoot you. Your boyfriend would take it very hard that he was feet away from you but couldn't save you."

"Emily," Nick shouted, smiling as he shoved his way toward her. She watched the change in Nick when he realized the danger. He reached behind for his gun.

Emily started to shake when Sabo put his gun against her temple. "Come any closer, Jenkins, and I'll kill her. You'll watch her blood spill over the bricks and not be able to do a damn thing."

"Sabo, it's over. You're surrounded," Agent Matthews shouted from behind. "Don't make this worse."

"I'll kill her if you come any closer, and then I'll take out as many as I can."

Someone in the crowd screamed. "Shooter!"

Panic ensued. People shoved and ran against each other to get away.

Emily was slammed against Sabo. Was this her chance?

"Don't try anything stupid." He pressed the gun against her hard, making her wince.

Nick inched closer.

"Don't move, Jenkins."

Emily saw Stella running toward her. Emily would have cried out to her dog but didn't want to call attention to her fur baby. Oh, God. He would shoot Stella.

Stella's little feet were moving rapidly. Her stout body went sailing into the air as she latched her teeth into Sabo's leg.

Startled by Stella's attack, he yelled and dropped the gun from Emily's temple. Emily turned and jabbed her fingers into his eyes. He staggered. "You bitch."

Emily hit the ground with Nick covering her. The gunshot reverberated in her ears.

"Oh, my God." She pushed on Nick, who didn't budge. "Darling, Nick. Are you shot?"

"My God, he had a gun." Nick was pale, and his hand was shaking as he ran it along her face. "He will never hurt you again."

Stella ran to Emily and started licking her face. All Emily could do was laugh and cry at the same time.

Nick lifted her to her feet. Emily bent and picked up Stella. And both she and Stella were wrapped in Nick's arms.

Unable to find words, Emily finally gulped. "My heroes."

CHAPTER TWENTY-THREE

Nick knocked before entering the master bedroom. Emily had taken Stella for a bath over an hour ago, wanting to wash any vestiges of evil men off her beloved Frenchie. Emily had discovered a microchip under Stella's collar when she took off the collar to discard it. The Serbians had the information the entire time. Nick was happy that they hadn't discovered the microchip for both Stella's and Emily's sakes. He didn't want Emily to suffer any more than she already had.

If he were really honest, he was the one who wasn't coping. He needed Emily—to touch her and be touched by her, to reassure himself that she was alive.

He hadn't recovered from the sight of Sabo's gun pressed against Emily's temple. He'd never forget how close he'd come to losing her today. Sabo, an agent trained to kill, was desperate and cornered. Nick's gut clenched at the thought of a totally different scenario without Stella's intervention.

"Emily, how are you and Stella doing?"

Stella, who had devoured Dean's liver pâté, showed no sign of maltreatment and was definitely doing well. Snoring on her back, Stella sprawled on the king-size bed. Saving her owner had tuckered out the little heroine.

Emily opened the bathroom door, wearing every man's fantasy—a tiny, red, lace negligee that hugged her curves.

As all the blood left his brain, Nick staggered, reeling in shock.

Primal lust sped through him. Like Stella, Emily was well and very much alive.

The light behind her silhouetted every glorious inch of her luscious body. Her damp hair fell around her shoulders in all its silky glory.

"You take my breath away. I'll never get used to how beautiful you are, Emily Elizabeth Hewitt." She gutted him, almost knocking his knees out from beneath him.

She sauntered toward him, her hips swaying in a rhythm that matched his pumping blood.

"Reeves told you my middle name?"

Nick's hands were shaking, his body close to the breaking point, and he hadn't even touched her.

All he could do was stare with his mouth wide open. Was he drooling? The racy outfit hit the top of her thighs, and the cut was so low it barely covered her breasts. Her erect nipples were puckered against the clinging silk.

"Nick?" Her tone had gone husky.

"You know what you're doing to me, don't you?" He demonstrated an inch with his fingers. "I'm this far from taking you against the wall." His voice rumbled in his chest as his dick throbbed.

"My middle name?"

He tried to tame the beast that now was painfully hard against his zipper. He focused on her words, reminding himself that Emily had been held at gunpoint this afternoon. She needed a tender and loving partner, not one who was wild and out of control.

He backed away, trying to make his brain work. "I read everything I could about you. I watched every YouTube video you've made, bought every CD. I tortured myself. I never stopped wanting you."

She stepped closer. Her damp hair's flowery fragrance, mixed with her woman's musky scent, enveloped him. "I never stopped wanting you either. You tortured me for four months, leaving me alone. I'm going to punish you for making me wait."

Nick's brain and body went into a frenzy, his dick lurching

against his jeans. Erotic images flooded his mind. He'd take her punishment like a man.

She slid her palms up his thighs to his belt buckle.

"You're going to drive me crazy, aren't you?"

"Maybe." She eased his zipper down, carefully opening the front of his jeans so she could reach his boxers. His erection strained against the fabric.

She ran one fingertip down his length before she released him from his boxers and wrapped her delicate hand around him.

"I've missed you, Nick. I've missed this—us together like this."

He was already out of control. His plan was to comfort and hold her after her traumatic day, explain his reasons for not pursuing her, and then make slow tender love. Was this Emily's way of taking control after everything she had been through? He didn't want to take that from her, but he wouldn't last. He needed to make it good for her.

"Please, Emily, I'm begging. Can you torture me later? Will you let me make us both happy? And then you can punish me any way you want." He stomped down the need to grab her. He slowly ran his finger along the edge of her negligee. "Please let me touch you."

Her face was flushed, and her lips parted in little pants. She gave a slight nod.

Her full breasts filled his palms with their sweet weight, just like he remembered.

"I didn't get to touch you in the kitchen. That night I lay in bed remembering how good your breasts felt in my hands and how I wanted to take you against the wall, fast and hard."

He ran his finger across her nipples. They puckered into hard nubs. Nick loved how she squirmed against him and how her breathing hitched when he tweaked them.

"And I regretted that I didn't feel you inside me, stretching me, like the time in the shower in Sausalito."

He had jerked off after the kitchen episode, envisioning taking her, remembering how wild she had been in the shower.

"I wanted you too—all hard and desperate."

He wrapped an arm around her waist and pulled her against his body. Her every curve pressed against him, teasing him. "Emily, I'm barely in control. It isn't the way I want our first time after how I've screwed up. I want you to be treated the way you deserve."

"Having you out of control is perfect—not thinking, not protecting, but you as a man, needing me as your mate, your woman. Not the responsible US Marine captain, but Nick Jenkins, the man who needs my love."

Emily, her head and shoulders thrown back, her mane of dark curls flowing around him, was like an avenging goddess. She was a force to be reckoned with, and he was the man who'd step up.

"I was so bitter and exhausted when I came to Sausalito. And there you were, all light and joy. I've been lost without you."

She cupped his face into her hand. "I'm here now. And I'm not leaving, no matter what crazy ass ideas you get about protecting me from yourself. Take me how you would have if we hadn't been interrupted. How you fantasized."

He slanted his mouth over hers and kissed her with everything he had while he walked her back until she reached the bedroom wall. He gripped both her hands in one of his and forced them over her head, opening her to his stare, his touch.

"I've dreamed about punishing you for making me want a life I could never have with you. For ruining me for any other woman or any other future without you." He kissed her, stroking his tongue against hers before he lifted her against the wall.

She clasped her hands behind his neck and locked her ankles at the small of his back. Nick shifted his hold, lifting her, aligning their bodies for the perfect fit. Heat burned through him. In that moment, he felt as if he had been cold all his life until Emily.

She slid onto the head of his shaft before enveloping him in her blazing grip. As he penetrated deeper, she gasped, and her head fell against his shoulder, her nails digging through his shirt.

"God, Emily, you feel so good." Her scent and her moans intoxicated him, making his head spin. Her eyes were wide, her face and her chest flushed as she rode him into heaven. He was spellbound, expanded in time watching, feeling her pleasure both of them. He was lost in her sensuality, the wonders of Emily taking him for the ride of a lifetime.

When she threw her head back and gripped him as if she'd never let go, he lost all control. He thrust faster, harder into her, taking her to the sweet place. With a cry, she surged closer. He wasn't going to last, but he could feel her beginning to tighten around him.

"Kiss me," she demanded.

He thrust one last time as he devoured her mouth, sucking her scream, absorbing her release into his soul as he lost himself in ecstasy.

Emily was limp in his arms, a sheen of perspiration covering her skin and her damp hair beginning to curl. He lightly pressed his lips to her forehead, to her eyelids, and then to her lips.

"Emily Elizabeth Hewitt." He was winded from this joyful sprint.

"I don't know your full name. Are you 'Nick' or 'Nicholas'?"

She dropped her head on his shoulder; her eyes remained closed.

"Nicholas Bergen Jenkins. Scandinavian."

"Mmm." Her warm lips pressed against his throat.

He lifted and carried her to the bed, loving the way she melted against him. He pulled back the covers and gently placed her on the sheets. Boneless, she fell on the bed, her red negligee riding up to the top of her thighs.

His dick hardened at the sight. Primal possession surged. He rebuked himself for wanting her again. He hadn't taken off his pants, but he was ready for an encore. She'd tossed his battle plan aside. He figured he'd tell her about his hearing loss before they made love. He wanted her to be informed, to give her a choice, not act out his fantasy.

He stripped off his clothes and climbed into bed. He pulled her against his chest, pushing her hair from her eyes. He kissed the tip of her nose.

Stella rolled from her back to her stomach but didn't wake.

Emily scooted closer, intertwining her leg with Nick's. He explored her round hip, the indentation, and the smooth skin of her thigh.

"It was better than the shower in Sausalito." She ran a fingertip down his chest. "Not that I'm complaining about the time in Sausalito. I think we should try the shower here for comparison. Maybe every shower in every room?"

"Emily, before we go any further, I have to explain. I didn't know that guarding you would end so abruptly. I thought I had time to tell you everything. And then I couldn't. I didn't want to ruin the memory of those days, and you were leaving for Asia... These are all dumb excuses. I was a damn coward. And you're right, I didn't give you a chance. In my job, I'm used to making the hard decisions...without regard for feelings."

She fingered the hair on his chest.

"What do you mean before we go any further? What is going through your crazy mind? Didn't we just prove to each other we're a perfect fit? I've never felt this connection before with anyone."

"It was wrong to tell you I love you without explaining why I didn't contact you. I wanted to tell you why I tried to avoid becoming involved with you. But seeing the Serbian put his hands on you in the dog park, I had to tell you that I love you. And today, with Sabo... Emily, I'll do whatever I can to make this work for us. But if you decide you'd rather not have a future with me, I'll walk away and never bother you again."

She pulled on his chest hair. "Nicholas Bergen Jenkins. Nothing is going to stop me from loving you unless you tell me you have a wife and three children." Her eyes were dancing with mischief.

"This isn't a joke." This was harder than anything he had ever done, including walking away from her the first time. Now, he knew he'd never recover.

"I was discharged from the marines because of a permanent hearing loss from an IED explosion. I'm damaged goods. No one knows how much worse it will get. There is no known treatment. You would be with a man who eventually might not be able to hear your music."

"Nick, darling." She propped herself up on one elbow to see him better. "I don't know much about hearing loss. But I know a lot about you. And I don't believe for a minute that you'll allow a hearing loss to get in the way of a full and wonderful life."

"But what about your music? I didn't realize it at the time, but I fell in love with you watching you practice the cello. I've been trained to read body language. I never witnessed anything quite like your gift. You transcend the instrument and become one with the music. I wanted to be part of your life, to watch the rapture spread across your face as you sent joy into the world. To forget all the violence, all the horrible things I've witnessed. But it felt wrong to bring my darkness to your light."

Emily stared into his eyes. She pressed her hand against his chest.

"When I look at you, I don't see a man filled with darkness. I see a man who is filled with love. A man who loves his brothers, his uncle, his mother, his country, and me. A man of courage and honor who is willing to sacrifice his happiness to protect others. I'll always play music, but I'm tired of touring, always on the move, in new cities with different people. It gets old. I want a more normal life."

"But I might eventually not be able to hear your concerts."

"Hearing aids won't work?"

He shrugged. "I haven't looked into them."

Emily climbed on top of his chest, her breasts barely covered by the red silk. "Nick, you're willing to sacrifice what we have because you don't want to wear a hearing aid?"

He gazed into her loving eyes. "No, I want you to have a choice if you want a man who will need hearing aids."

"I don't want 'a man' with hearing aids. I want you with all your faults and imperfections." She rubbed her heat against him. "There are parts of you I like exactly how they are."

"Are you sure? Because I will never walk away. You're stuck with me."

Laughing, Emily wrapped her hand around his erection "I think you'll do just fine."

He flipped her over and loomed over her. "I love you. And I'm going to taste every inch of you. No rushing to the finish. But let's get you out of this."

He lifted the negligee over her head, needing to pause and feel her soft, smooth skin.

He proceeded to slowly kiss his way down Emily's body when he was struck that she hadn't seemed shocked by his admission.

"You already knew about my hearing loss, didn't you?"

Emily scooted up to the headboard. Her cheeks pinked. "I did. Carter mentioned it on the phone when we were on our way to the airport."

"Did Reeves tell you that Jordan wants me to go into a gene therapy experimental study?"

"No. I don't think Reeves knows." Emily puffed out her lower lip in a fake pout. "Does this mean you'll be able to hear me scream your name without a hearing aid?"

"Honey, I'll always be able to hear you. Let me show you right now."

He pulled her legs to the edge of the bed. He knew exactly how to make Emily scream.

EPILOGUE

Lying on her side, Emily snuggled under the covers, trying to get warm. She slid in search of Nick's hot body. The man was an incredible heat source.

She rolled over to find a cold, empty space. She pulled the covers up to her ears, wishing Nick was there to warm her. Where had he gone? She needed Nick and a coffee chaser if she had to get out of bed. She wanted to stay here all day with Nick and not face the CIA, Reeves, the police. The list went on.

The door flew open. Nick carried a tray while Stella danced in circles by his legs. The rich aroma of coffee and bacon filled the room.

Nick's hair was tousled, his morning beard pronounced on his angular chin. His gray sweats hung on his lean hips, and he was bare chested, exposing sculpted pecs and abs. The man's body, like her cello, was a perfect finely tuned and beautiful instrument.

"How are you feeling, sleepyhead?" His warm eyes searched her face.

Nick, all sexy and drool worthy, unsure and concerned for her well-being, created an intoxicating feeling for a woman.

Was he worried that she couldn't handle his insatiable needs? Heat flashed through her, thinking of what a demanding lover Nick had been. They had barely gotten any sleep. But last night was markedly different from their night in Sausalito.

Last night Nick never stopped telling her how much he loved her, how much he needed her. With their mutual outpouring of feelings, their lovemaking changed from combustible chemistry to tender intimacy.

All she could do was grin. She was a woman in love and a woman loved.

"This feels like Christmas morning."

Nick's smile, lighting up his face, made him look younger, how he must have looked as a boy. Emily planned to ask his mother to share pictures of him growing up. She wanted to know every detail about Nick Jenkins.

"That's my line—how I'm looking forward to unwrapping my favorite present."

"I think you already did the unwrapping." Emily nodded toward the red camisole on the floor.

"You in that red get-up is better than any Christmas present I've ever received. I'm hoping you'll bring it to Hawaii."

He placed the tray loaded with coffee, French toast, bacon, and fruit on the bed. He leaned over and took her mouth, his lips demanding for her to open to him. His tongue searched, sliding and seeking.

Heat and need flashed through Emily as she reciprocated in a dance of tongues.

Stella began a dirge-like howl for being ignored.

Nick chuckled and bent to lift Stella onto the bed.

"You stay." Nick used his stern voice. Stella smiled and laid on the end of the bed. It was all an act. Stella would soon start her slow stomach crawl to get to the tray.

Emily plumped the pillow behind her back. "I'm planning on buying a few bikinis when we get to Hawaii. I don't think I'll need much more. Will I?"

She and Nick had decided that, after everything they had gone through, they would take his brothers' gift and spend the month on Kauai in the Deans' waterfront house. They planned on spending the time alone, with no interruptions from brothers or team members.

"You in a bikini on the white sand of Kauai… How did I get to be such a lucky bastard? I wish you could've heard Finn's voice when I told him this morning that I planned to use the brothers' intervention."

Nick's grin made her stomach do flip-flops. How could a man be that gorgeous?

"His voice lowered, and he used his Navy Seal 'this is a serious mission' voice. 'I'm glad to hear that you see the need. It will do you good. It's only because we care.' I tried to let him go on and dig himself deeper, but I started to crack up."

"Did he threaten any of my favorite body parts?" Emily rubbed Nick's erection, tenting in his sweats, so close and so prominent.

"If you want to eat your French toast, you have to stop." Nick grabbed her hand and brought it to his mouth. He licked her palm, making her giggle.

"Talking about brothers, I'm surprised Reeves hasn't appeared yet this morning."

"Reeves and the guys just left. I had to fight off Tanner from claiming your French toast." Nick lifted the tray and placed it on her lap.

"All the men were here? And I slept through the noise." Emily lifted the mug to take her first sip of morning coffee.

"I tired you out, honey." The smugness in Nick's voice didn't bother her one bit. She enjoyed every minute of his efforts.

"How did Reeves react to all the men's smirks and backslapping about you getting lucky last night?"

Nick jostled her on the bed and sat close, their hips bumping. He leaned forward and smoothed her hair from her face. "I do feel very lucky, but not because of some male bullshit. Lucky because you gave me a second chance after I was a complete dumbass. The men would never demean you that way. They know I'd kick their asses."

"I'm sort of surprised Reeves didn't wake me up."

"He wanted to…"

Emily would have liked to have been a fly on the wall to watch Nick handle Reeves.

"He wanted you to know that the bullet from Charles's and Yuen Li's bodies match the gun of your bald driver. The guy is going down."

"I hope that will give both families some relief. Will the CIA tell Yuen Li's family what a hero Yuen Li was?" Emily would grieve the kind and generous men for a long time. She would think of a way to honor their memory with her music.

"Funny, you should ask. Agent Matthews called to inform us that the microchip identified all of Sabo's contacts in China. The information will allow the CIA to stop the conduit of our country's secrets to China. Matthews also apologized for his poor professional judgment concerning your safety. I'm not sure who was behind the reprimand, but Matthews is being transferred to another office."

"You've had a very busy morning. You might have to come back to bed."

Nick stood and slipped off his sweats, his erection impressive and forefront in Emily's view. "This is a test of your hunger. Me or the French toast?"

Her spirit buoyed by the very serious Nick Jenkins acting playful.

Emily tried to sound serious but was unable to keep the playful lilt out of her voice. "I'm thinking both. I've heard maple syrup makes everything sweeter."

Dear Readers,

Thank you for reading *Mission: Impossible to Forget*. I hope you like Nick and Emily as much as I do. I hated to see their story end. It's part of the reason I love writing series, so my characters can keep reappearing. I have big plans for Nick's next career.

I wanted to give you some insight into my choice to give Nick a hearing loss and to make Emily a cellist.

In developing my *Impossible Mission* Series, I became very aware of the high incidence of hearing damage in Military Personnel from training exercises, weapons, and large vehicular engines and tanks. A study by the *Journal of General Internal Medicine* found that 16.4-26.6% of male veterans of the Afghanistan War and the Iraq War suffer from serious hearing loss and tinnitus. That same study found that 7.3-13.4% of female veterans had hearing loss.

I wanted to increase awareness of this subtle, possibly silent, hidden injury. Hearing loss can progress from a nuisance to a disability affecting multi facets of one's life—difficulty in maintaining social situations, isolation from friends and family.

My character, Nick, struggles with his diagnosis and his subsequent medical discharge from the Marines. His denial and aversion to hearing aids is one possibility of coping with the hidden impairment.

I've always loved the cello and have fantasized about learning to play the instrument. I know the challenge of mastering an instrument and am fortunate to have the writer's option—creating a character who is a gifted cellist. I tried hard not to include too many music references but in Emily's world, I imagined she would hear and think in music. I loved listening to the music as I wrote Emily's story.

I've included YouTube links to a few of the pieces I've mentioned in the book:

Emily's favorite cello music played by Yo-Yo Ma.
Bach Suite #1
https://www.youtube.com/watch?v=1prweT95Mo0

Emily refers to her attraction to Nick as music by Ludovico Einaudi. *Tu Sei* is played by Mr. & Mrs. Cello.
https://www.youtube.com/watch?v=-2BUX9HaT0k

And Emily relates closely to Adam Hurst and his compositions. Adam Hurst's *Remaining*.
https://www.youtube.com/watch?v=1CZ0WyN-D8g

Enjoy an excerpt from

MISSION:
impossible to
RESIST

THE
IMPOSSIBLE
MISSION
SERIES

BESTSELLING AUTHOR
JACKI DELECKI

CHAPTER ONE

Jordan Dean couldn't catch a break. There was no escaping the unwanted and, more than likely uninvited, guests this evening. Now Morley Townsend was in the receiving line. Her sister would never have invited Jordan's ex, because Sophie knew exactly how Jordan felt about the possessive, self-absorbed millionaire. Morley was probably here as part of another of their father's elaborate realignments of the people he saw as chess pieces.

How could an evening dedicated to global peace end up seething with such hostility, resentment, and homicidal urges? And she'd only been here about twenty minutes.

Jordan pivoted—intent on escaping to the balcony before Morley spotted her—and walked straight into a very big, very solid, very muscular wall. The sudden impact set her wobbling. The way this evening was going, she should have stayed in her flats.

The solid, muscular wall grabbed her elbows with hot, rough hands and held on until she was steadier.

"Running from a fight?" His voice was polished, smooth, and smoky, like the fifty-year-old Scottish single malt whisky Morley liked to go on about ad nauseam.

Jordan looked up…and up…into penetrating aquamarine eyes. A darker blue circle rimmed each iris, like a ring around an outer planet.

"Fight?" Her voice came out high-pitched and strangled.

He leaned closer and confided as an aside, as if they were well-acquainted, "First the itsy woman you nailed with your shoe. I was hoping to see more. And now, from the way you're high-tailing it away from the door, I'd say you're avoiding Mr. Zippity Slick…" He tipped his head toward her ex.

She twisted around to see Morley run his hand over his perfect hair, held in place by his designer clay pomade.

"Zippity Slick?" She could barely contain an unladylike snort, and the simultaneous urge to burst into hysterical giggles. Not the image Morley was aiming for with his pricey hair product.

Her muscular wall grinned, softening the razor-sharp angles of his cheekbones and making his light eyes even lighter. "An angry ex?"

Jordan's mind raced, trying to keep up with their off-kilter exchange. This was the strangest conversation she could ever remember having, made more distracting because here was a man who easily put Chris Hemsworth to shame, with his shredded body and *blue-flame-of-intensity* eyes surrounded by inky black lashes.

What he was he playing at?

"Nailed it, didn't I?" His warm, minty breath brushed against her cheek when he chuckled.

Jordan stared up into the enormous man's piercing eyes, practically baking in his heat and virility. "Let go of me, or I'll call over my bodyguard." She hated that her voice came out puny and tinny.

He waited a second too long to release her arms, then moved in close, too close, further invading her private space. "You've got to be kidding." He crossed his arms and grinned, his eyes alight with amusement and a challenge. "Go ahead. Call him."

She quickly scanned the hall, looking for Harry and the crew who guarded her and her sister 24/7.

"Your bodyguard is sick. And you haven't noticed that he isn't here, have you?"

Her heart kicked into tachycardia speeding out of control. "Harry is sick?"

"Not Harry…Pete, the man who regularly guards you. You didn't notice, did you?"

Jordan searched for Pete, a middle-aged, retired policeman who was a regular member of her security detail. He hadn't been at his post, which this evening was at the door downstairs, vetting everyone who entered the building.

Relief surged through her when she spotted Harry, who was standing by the door wearing his rumpled navy blue suit and the burgundy Armani tie she gave him for his birthday.

Mr. Mountain shook his head. "Unbelievable. You have absolutely no situational awareness."

"Shows how much you know." Situational awareness. She had it in spades—no, in sharp-edged diamonds. She was hyper-aware of Sophie's discomfort when greeting Rob Boyer, an associate of their father's and married man who had been hitting on Sophie since she was sixteen...and of Laura Stuliley cornering Sarah Sorenson's husband...and the tension between the elderly Dr. Levin and his hottie young bride.

Jordan wanted to defend herself, but she had a feeling he wouldn't be impressed.

And she had noticed Pete was absent from the downstairs entrance earlier, before her little tête–à–tête with Georgette. But, honestly, how much risk could there be while socializing in a private room, in a private club, guarded by her family's private security firm? Especially since Harry was here.

And who the hell was this man to criticize her...situational awareness...anyway?

"Who are you? I know you weren't invited tonight."

"Stand out, do I?" The edge was back in his voice, his granite jaw getting tighter with every word.

Interesting. Mr. Chiseled was sensitive?

Mission: Impossible to Resist is available in ebook and paperback from your favorite online retailer.

Jacki Delecki is a bestselling romantic suspense author whose stories are filled with heart-pounding adventure, danger, intrigue, and romance. Her books have consistently received rave reviews, and AN INNER FIRE was chosen as an Editor's Selection by *USA Today*. Currently, she has three series: the contemporary romantic suspense Impossible Mission, featuring Special Force operatives; Grayce Walters, contemporary romantic suspense following a Seattle animal acupuncturist with a nose for crime; and the Code Breakers, Regency suspense set against the backdrop of the Napoleonic Wars. Delecki's stories reflect her lifelong love affair with the arts and history. When not writing, she volunteers for Seattle's Ballet and Opera Companies, and leads children's tours of Pike Street Market.

To learn more about Jacki and her books and to be the first to hear about giveaways join her newsletter found on her website. Follow her on Facebook Jacki Delecki; Twitter @jackidelecki; Bookbub jacki-delecki; Goodreads Jacki_Delecki.

http://www.JackiDelecki.com

9 780998 527659